THE
UNICORN
IN THE
BARN

www.hmhco.com

The text was set in Minion Pro.

Library of Congress Cataloging-in-Publication Data
Names: Ogburn, Jacqueline K., author. | Green, Rebecca, illustrator.
Title: The unicorn in the barn / written by Jacqueline Ogburn ; with
illustrations by Rebecca Green.
Description: New York, New York : Houghton Mifflin Harcourt, [2017] |
Summary: Fifth-grader Eric's life transforms when he encounters a unicorn
in the woods around Chinaberry Creek and discovers a special veterinary
clinic that cares for "supernatural exotic patients."
Identifiers: LCCN 2016014202 | ISBN 9780544761124 (hardcover)
Subjects: | CYAC: Unicorns—Fiction. | Veterinary hospitals—Fiction.
| Supernatural—Fiction. | BISAC: JUVENILE FICTION / Animals
/ Mythical. | JUVENILE FICTION / Family / Multigenerational.
| JUVENILE FICTION / Fantasy & Magic. | JUVENILE
FICTION / Social Issues / Death & Dying. | JUVENILE
FICTION / Social Issues / Friendship.
Classification: LCC PZ7.O3317 Un 2017 | DDC [Fic]—dc23
LC record available at https://lccn.loc.gov/2016014202

Manufactured in the United States of America
DOC 10 9 8 7 6 5 4 3 2
4500663716

THE UNICORN IN THE BARN

by
Jacqueline K. Ogburn

illustrated by
Rebecca Green

HOUGHTON MIFFLIN HARCOURT
Boston   New York

To my Uncle Jackie,
who has always loved animals
—J.K.O.

To Mori and Junie B,
my own two magical creatures
—R.G.

Not to hurt our humble brethren is our first duty to them, but to stop there is not enough. We have a higher mission: to be of service to them whenever they require it.

— *St. Francis of Assisi*

CHAPTER ONE

MY DAD ALWAYS TOLD ME, "Never surprise somebody swinging a hammer; something is liable to get smashed." Still, when I first saw Allegra Brancusi, I couldn't help myself. She was slapping a No Trespassing sign up against a tree — *my* tree. The one with my treehouse in it.

"Hey, stop that!" I shouted. She was raising the hammer to drive in the nail and, sure enough, that hammer went flying back over her shoulder and nearly clipped me on the arm.

She whirled around and glared at me. "You

shouldn't sneak up on people like that. It's rude." It's not like I had done a commando crawl through the bushes for the sole purpose of sneaking up on her. I had just walked down the path like always. Not my fault I couldn't see her until I got to the top of the ridge. "I'm posting these signs and you can't stop me," she said, shaking the yellow-and-black poster in my face.

"I can see that. What I want to know is why. This is Harper's Woods and I'm a Harper. That's my tree-house up there and you can't keep me out." I glared back.

"Well, Mr. A. Harper, it should be called Brancusi Woods now and I'm Allegra Brancusi, that's why." She swung her arm out, using the poster as a pointer. "My mother bought this farm. She told me to post these No Trespassing signs on this side of our property, in a line starting at that telephone pole."

The telephone pole was the third one down from our mailbox, next to the road at the bottom of the hill. It had a ring of yellow-and-black signs wrapped around it. There was a stretch of weeds that used to be a cornfield, and right behind it, the edge of the woods. Sure enough, a line of posters marked trees every few feet, up to where we were standing. She was right about where the property line started, but not about where it ran. I set her straight right then.

"So, Allegra Who-si, didn't your mom tell you about surveyor's stakes?" She shook her head. "Your property line starts at that pole, but it doesn't run straight up to the top of the ridge. See those stakes with the orange ribbons? That's where the line is." I pointed at the stake about fifty yards down the hill and to another stake ten feet beyond that and another beyond that. Her eyes followed my finger and she bit her bottom lip, looking uncertain now. "How do you know that?" she asked.

"I helped the surveyor set them out. We had to sell the farmhouse, but my dad promised we'd keep the top of this hill. Bobby Knapp did the surveying; you can ask him." I picked up the hammer and handed it back to her. "If anybody is trespassing here, it's you."

"Oh," she said, taking the hammer and poking it through a loop on the leg of her carpenter jeans. It was the first time I ever saw a girl do that—actually use one of those loops for what you're supposed to. She looked back at the line of stakes, then picked up her backpack and stuffed the poster back inside. "Fine," she said. "I'll ask my mom about the stakes."

"Yeah, well, you should check things out before you go hammering on other people's trees." I crossed my arms and waited.

"Whatever," she said, shrugging her backpack across her shoulder. She stomped off down the hill toward the big white farmhouse that used to be my grandmother's.

I grabbed on to the board nailed about four feet up the trunk and scrambled into my treehouse. It's not much to look at, but it's been my favorite place since I was six. It's a small wooden square stuck to the side of the tree, just big enough for me to stretch out in. I built up the sides to about three feet high and I have a tarp in it to keep the rain off my stuff. The boards are this nice silvery gray color now.

The best thing is, it's on this ridge, so you can see real well all around. It's the perfect place to watch everything. I can even see where the little creek runs to the north. When the wind is still, I can hear the water.

Down to the west is my house, a brick ranch. It's pretty close to the road, but still has a nice stand of trees curving around it, like the woods are holding the house in its arms. My dad built it when he married my mom. On the other side of the rise, farther back in the woods, sits the farmhouse with a wraparound porch and a bunch of outbuildings. My many-times great-granddaddy, Cletus Harper, built the front part, just two little rooms and a fireplace, near about two hundred years ago. Harpers have been adding on to it ever since.

I peered over the side to watch Allegra trudge down the path out of the woods and into the backyard of the farmhouse. When Grandma was living there, I must have walked that path at least four or five times a day. I hadn't been down it in months, not since Grandma had to move into the nursing home and we had to sell the farmhouse. The girl disappeared around the back corner of the house. I heard the screen door slam, so I guess she went inside.

After a few minutes, I figured she wasn't coming back, so I stretched out on the boards. I let my eyes close to little slits, until the leaves and patches of light looked like big white and green blotches moving just beyond my eyelashes.

I must've fallen asleep, because when I opened my eyes, everything was dark. The half-moon gave enough light to see some of the branches. Rising up on my knees, I shuffled around to look down at our house. My brother Steve's car wasn't in the carport.

He was
probably still
at work. Ghostly blue
light flickered from the den window. I guess Dad
fell asleep too, in front of the TV again. My stomach
growled. I had missed dinner, if anybody had both-
ered to fix it.

Leaves shushed and rustled over by the creek. It
sounded like something big and cautious, maybe a
deer, was passing. I just turned my head to look, so as
not to make any sound and spook it. Even the weak
lights from the house had dulled my night vision,

so I couldn't see anything at first. Then a pale shape moved near a clump of blackberry canes. It was too big to be a raccoon and too quiet to be a stray calf.

Maybe it was the white deer. People had talked about a white deer around here for ages, although nobody could say for sure if it was a buck or a doe. Every season, some hunter swore he shot it, but it always got away.

The boards creaked softly as I moved into a better position to watch. The animal stepped away from the underbrush, definitely the wrong size and shape for a calf. It came closer to the treehouse, moving slowly. My eyes had adjusted to the moonlight.

It wasn't a deer.

White and glowing, with slender legs and a long curved neck, at first I thought it was a pony. Then it raised its head and I knew. Ponies don't move so quietly through the woods. Ponies don't have coats that shimmer like a pearl. And there's never been a pony born with an ivory horn curling from the center of its forehead.

It was a unicorn.

It was the most beautiful thing I'd ever seen.

Looking at it, I got the most amazing feeling of comfort and happiness and excitement, all rolled up into one. Like when Grandma would sing me a lullaby, or when I smacked a baseball way out to left field, or when the air is charged, just before lightning strikes.

I had never seen anything so amazing. I could have sat there looking at it all night. Then I noticed a strange smell, like roses and pine and new turned dirt.

The unicorn picked its way carefully around the trees with a funny gait, two steps and a hop. Its head drooped and after each hop, it huffed, a sound almost like a snort. As it moved down the ridge, I realized that it was lame. The unicorn stumbled and I sucked in my breath, but it didn't fall. It reached the bottom of the hill. I wanted to help, but wild things are dangerous, especially when they're hurt. And what could be wilder than a unicorn?

Something so beautiful should be perfect; it shouldn't be hurting. I couldn't just watch it suffer. I started to climb down when it nickered, a long, low call.

A light flicked on inside the farmhouse; then the back porch light came on too. A tall lady walked out of the house and stopped in the yard. She beckoned to the unicorn, then pulled open the barn door and stood to one side. The unicorn stopped, caught in the light from the barn, glowing like the moon. I thought it might bolt. It stared at the lady for a long moment before dropping its head and limping through the door. Once it was safely inside, the lady slid the door shut.

CHAPTER TWO

WHEN THE DOOR CLOSED, everything dimmed. It wasn't just that the barn light was cut off. Suddenly everything looked watery and dingy, like the reflections in an old mirror where the silver backing has gone bad.

I glanced at my house. The TV still flickered. I climbed down from the treehouse and set out for the barn. My feet still knew the way in the dark, and made soft little padding sounds in the dirt.

At the edge of the woods, instead of going straight, I circled around the old chicken coop and tractor shed. I had heard that the lady who bought the farmhouse and some of the land was a vet, an animal doctor, and she planned to make a clinic downstairs. People wondered why she bought so much of the land if she wasn't going to farm, but it made sense now. I'd never heard of a vet who had unicorns for patients. There was a small window to the left of the barn door. If she was taking care of the unicorn, then she would be too busy to notice me if I peeked in there.

Carefully, I leaned on the windowsill and peered inside. The vet was squatting next to the unicorn, examining the bottom of its right front hoof. The creature was calm, studying the lady's face, listening to her talk. The lady acted just like she was explaining something to a person. I couldn't make out the words, but her tone was gentle and even. The unicorn huffed once and nodded as the vet reached for something in a black bag.

"OWWW!" Someone yanked my head back by

the hair, hard. I jabbed back with my elbow, connecting with something soft.

"Oof!" The grip on my hair let go. I whirled around, and was face-to-face with that girl Allegra. Holding her side where I'd poked her, she cut her eyes at me like I was something nasty she found in the sink.

"Who's trespassing now?" she demanded, shoving me in the chest so I fell back against the wall. I put up my hands to protect my face. "What do you think you're doing, sneaking around in the middle of the night?" she shrieked, slapping at me.

I tried to slide away, but it just seemed to make her madder and louder.

"Get out! Go away, sneak!" she yelled. Dad always told me not to hit girls, but I wasn't a bit sorry I had poked this one. Just wish I'd done it harder.

"I didn't do anything, you stupid girl," I yelled back. "I just wanted to make sure that unicorn is OK!"

Allegra gasped. "You aren't supposed to know

about that! It's a secret!" The barn door slid open and light poured over us.

"It's not a secret if he's already seen her. The unicorn will be fine and will be even better if you two keep quiet," the vet said. "Allegra, what's going on here? Who is this boy?" The lady put her hands on her hips and glared at us both. I straightened up and dropped my arms.

"I'm Eric Harper, ma'am," I said, glad I was able to answer before that girl jumped in. "I saw the unicorn come through the woods and I could tell it was hurt. Can you help it?" I shifted around, trying to catch sight of it, but it must have moved into one of the stalls. "Is it gonna be all right?"

The lady's face softened. "I think so, Eric," she said, holding out her right hand. "I'm Kris Brancusi, Dr. Brancusi. I see you've already met my daughter, Allegra. Any relation to Maggie Harper?"

"Yes, ma'am," I said as we shook hands. "She's my grandmother."

"So you probably know your way around this barn better than I do," she said. She stared at me hard. I could see she was considering what to do. "Come on in, see for yourself." She stepped back and motioned me inside.

"Mom!" Allegra cried. "What are you doing? You can't let him in here!" She grabbed for my arm, but I slipped past her and through the door.

I walked slowly down the aisle and stopped in front of the middle stall on the left. The unicorn looked at me calmly. I couldn't help but smile, the way you do at newborn puppies. A soft glow radiated from her, like warm moonlight. She held her right forefoot up off the floor as if it pained her. She gave a little hop and stretched out her nose to me. I touched her gently between the nostrils, where her muzzle was whiskery and velvety soft. Warmth rushed up my hand and through my whole body.

"We're going to take good care of you," I told her, stroking her nose, but not daring to touch that horn.

She turned her head slightly to look at me. She had greeny-brown eyes, like a ripening acorn. I could tell she understood every word. Then she huffed and backed away.

"What's wrong with her?" I asked. Allegra and her mother had come up beside me. That peaceful feeling coming from the unicorn must have touched Allegra too, because she wasn't glaring at me anymore.

"She's got some pus in her hoof from some sort of infection. I need to drain it first," Dr. Brancusi explained. She studied me for a moment, then turned back to the unicorn. "Allegra, get my blue box." The girl ran to get it.

Dr. Brancusi took something off a peg and held it for the unicorn to see. "I'm going to put this halter on you while I work. The halter won't hurt, but what I'll be doing to your hoof might. I don't want you to injure the kids or me by moving suddenly. Eric will hold this rope to keep your head still." She slipped a loop over the unicorn's ears and the bottom loop around her muzzle. "Oh, good girl. I bet you're not used to one of these, are you?" The unicorn shook her head, then stood quietly.

Dr. Brancusi motioned me over. "Stand here and hold the halter while I work on that hoof." She looped the rope around a peg. I took hold of the end and stood where she said. "Keep some tension on it, but don't jerk it." She fastened another length of rope on the other side, then looped it around another hook, so the unicorn's head was held steady between the two.

The strange sweet smell was so strong I just wanted to close my eyes and drink it. Swirls of color ran along the horn—shimmery, like oil on water. The point looked mighty sharp.

Dr. Brancusi crouched down and lifted the unicorn's foot. Gently, she touched the underside of the hoof, the soft part, which was puffy, with a dark splotch in the middle. The unicorn sucked in a big breath, but held still. The vet ran her hand up the unicorn's leg, then held it while looking at her watch. Allegra came back with what looked like a big tackle box and set it down at the front of the stall.

"I need the lancet," Dr. Brancusi said. Allegra opened the box, which was full of syringes, small sharp tools, and lots of little bottles, and took out a thin scalpel. Her mother took the instrument and held it up so the unicorn could see.

"I'm going to make a cut to drain the infection. This is made from titanium; it doesn't have any iron. It may hurt a bit, but then your hoof can begin to heal. Understand?" At first I thought she was talking to me, but when the unicorn nodded, I realized my mistake.

She took a firmer grip on the hoof, resting it on her leg, then with a flick, she cut along the inside. Greenish-yellow goo oozed out and dripped onto her blue jeans. A sour stink hit my nose and the unicorn's too, because a shiver ran across her neck.

The vet wiped the hoof with some gauze that Allegra handed her, then with another pad that came away with streaks of red mixed in with the green and yellow. She squeezed on the hoof some more and the unicorn gave a little grunt.

"Tweezers," she said, holding out her hand toward Allegra.

Allegra wiped a pair of tweezers with a cloth that stank of disinfectant. The vet gently probed the cut with them. Another shiver skittered across the unicorn's skin. I couldn't see very well because the doctor was leaning so close over the hoof.

"Got it," she said. Sitting back on her heels, she raised up the tweezers. Gripped in the tips was a tiny piece of metal. "Looks like a bit of old barbed wire, don't you think?"

Allegra leaned in to see. "It looks rusty. It probably does have iron and that's why it got infected." The unicorn bent her head to peer at it, too, and seemed to nod in agreement.

"What does iron have to do with it?" I asked. "Most animals get infections when they step on a rusty nail. People too, for that matter."

"Many supernatural creatures are allergic to iron. Some can tolerate it, but for some it's like poison and can be deadly," Dr. Brancusi explained. "Unicorns have magical healing powers, so I suppose they rarely get sick. The iron probably suppressed her healing ability. I've never had the chance to treat a unicorn before, so I'm not entirely sure." She picked up the hoof again. "Hand me the Animalintex and some Melolin."

Allegra gave her little packages of stuff that her mother spread on the hoof. Then she packed more gauze on it. I could see how well they worked together, each doing her tasks and not getting in the other's way. Allegra pulled out a roll of some stretchy material, which her mother wrapped around the foot. Then Allegra snipped off a length of duct tape and that was the top layer of wrapping. Dr. Brancusi was careful to cover only the hoof, and not catch any of the hair or skin under the sticky tape. Dad always says you can fix anything with duct tape, but I don't think this is what he had in mind.

The unicorn held her leg so the front of the hoof rested on the ground. Dr. Brancusi stood, then stroked the unicorn's neck. She swept her hands across her back, making little soothing sounds. "I should give you a shot now. Some antibiotics for the infection and a tetanus shot. But you look pregnant, and I don't want to give you a treatment that might hurt your baby." She said this looking straight at the unicorn, who again nodded her head in agreement.

"The good news is, this won't hurt at all," she said, taking a stethoscope out of the box. "It might feel cold." She rubbed her hand on the end of the little disk, then stuck the tips in her ears. Hunkering down on her heels next to the unicorn's side, she placed the disk on the rib cage. She listened for a moment, slid the scope lower, and then moved it again.

Even I could now see that the unicorn's belly stuck out more on the sides than her ribs and that it hung down low.

"You have a nice strong heartbeat. Now I'm trying to hear the baby." She moved the disk again, more under the belly, then frowned a bit.

"What's wrong?" asked Allegra.

"Hush." Still frowning, Dr. Brancusi moved the disk to a new place, then back, then to a third place and back again. She sat back on her heels, petting the unicorn's belly.

"Well, honey, I'm going to hold off on the shots for a while," she said to the unicorn. "You're definitely expecting, and I think it's twins!"

"Twins!" Allegra cried. "Are you sure?"

"There are two rapid heartbeats coming from the belly."

"That's so cool!" I said.

"You want to hear them?" Dr. Brancusi asked me. Allegra glared. I could tell she thought she should go first. Her mother motioned me over and when I crouched down, she hooked the stethoscope around my neck. I slid the earbuds in. She put the disk back on the unicorn's ribs.

"You should be able to hear the mother's heartbeat now." And I could hear it, big *da-dum, da-dum, da-dum* sounds. The smell of earth and roses was real strong, and I could feel a big old grin spread across my face. The vet moved the disk lower down on the unicorn's belly, which had more pink showing through the white of her coat. "Now one of the babies," she said.

It took a moment; then I could hear a fainter but faster beat, *da-da, da-da, da-da-dum.* She moved the disk farther underneath.

"Do you hear the second one?"

Leaning in, I closed my eyes so I could focus on just my ears. *Da-da, da-da, da-da;* then, faint like a second voice in the choir, I could hear a second heartbeat behind the first, *da-de-da, da-de-dum.* I

put my hand, real gentle, close to the disk. The unicorn's skin was warm and firm, like muscle, and didn't have a lot of give, like my belly. I couldn't feel anything moving.

"Wow," I said softly. Dr. Brancusi smiled at me.

"My turn," snarled Allegra, poking me in the side with her knee. I let her take my place and stood next to the unicorn's head. I could tell when Allegra heard the babies. She smiled, and her face was soft-looking, almost pretty.

"It *is* twins," she said. Then her eyes got big and worried. "But aren't twins dangerous for horses?"

Dr. Brancusi nodded, then explained to me, "Horses don't have enough room in their bodies to carry twins successfully, so usually one is aborted or dies. But with unicorns, who knows?" She ran her hands along the unicorn's side. "She's built a little different from a horse. Her chest is broader, and the rib cage seems larger. The pelvis is different, more like a goat. There might be room in there for two."

The vet moved up to her head and scratched the unicorn just behind the ears. "All done for now. You'll need to stay here for a while. The dressing needs to be changed twice a day for seven days. I also want to watch for signs that the infection isn't clearing up. If not, we'll have to give you shots anyway, so it won't spread through your system. Understand?"

The unicorn made what sounded like a sigh and nodded her head to show that she understood. The vet unhooked the ropes and took the halter off the unicorn's head.

"I also want to see you frequently while you are carrying these twins. I'll help you in any way I can, and your babies too." The unicorn nuzzled Dr. Brancusi on the arm.

The vet was giving me a hard look, like she was making up her mind about something. "She's going to need to be kept hidden here in the barn, maybe for months. Allegra, you know I depend on you, but I think we could use some extra help."

"Mom," Allegra said, tugging on her mother's arm. "You can't mean that. We can manage just fine; we don't need him."

"Sweetie, I think we do. We haven't had a large animal to board before. She's going to need a lot of care." Dr. Brancusi drew herself up. I'd been so focused on the unicorn, I hadn't noticed how big she was, almost as tall as my dad. With a stern expression that would have done a Sunday school teacher proud, she said, "Eric, you did well tonight. We can use your help, but this part of my practice must be kept secret. You can't tell anyone, not even your parents. These creatures come to me for healing, not to be tormented or turned into a freak show. Can we trust you?" Allegra didn't look too happy, but didn't say anything.

The unicorn turned her head and gazed at me with a big acorn-colored eye. She wanted me to agree, I could tell.

"I swear, I won't tell a soul," I said. "I'll do anything you say, whatever she needs." The unicorn rubbed my shoulder with her nose, being careful not to poke me with her horn.

I stuck out my hand and Dr. Brancusi shook it.

"Great. You're hired," she said.

CHAPTER THREE

OF COURSE, IT WASN'T THAT SIMPLE. I was only in the fifth grade, so this meant I was hired the way kids are who work as babysitters or lawn mowers. Dad had to be in on it. He just didn't have to know about the more unusual parts of the job.

Dad was asleep on the couch when I got home that night. Keeping real quiet, I made myself a peanut butter and banana sandwich, then cleaned up the kitchen. I heard Steve come in later. I could hardly sleep, thinking about the unicorn—how she looked, how soft her nose was, that amazing smell she had.

Bacon was sizzling when I woke up in the morning. My room is closest to the kitchen, a considerable benefit to my mind, as I get all the cooking smells first. Dad was curled over a cup of coffee and Steve was frying eggs when I bopped into the kitchen. Steve had been fixing breakfast a lot since he started working at the Chinaberry Diner. Sunlight came shining in big blocks through the window over the sink. It was Saturday and I was going to see the unicorn again.

I scooped up three slices of bacon and caught the toast as it popped up. Lifting the plate through the air like a fancy waiter, I swooped to the table. "Your breakfast is served, mis-sewer," I said. Dad quirked his lips in a little smile as he lifted his coffee cup.

I poured juice and got out the butter and jelly while Steve finished two more eggs.

"I've got a job!" I said.

"Now what kind of fool would give a job to an eleven-year-old?" Steve snorted.

"Dr. Brancusi wants me to help out with her veterinary practice, just easy stuff, like getting water and food for the animals, maybe doing some yard work," I told them. "It's only a couple of hours a day. I can do it after school and on weekends. She said she'd pay me."

Dad clunked down his coffee mug. "Dr. Who?"

"Dr. Brancusi—you know, the lady who bought the farmhouse?"

"That's what I thought you said." Dad leaned back in his chair, giving me a hard look. "You want to work for that woman?"

Dad's lips were in a tight line. Maybe I should've waited until after breakfast to bring this up. I was suddenly scared that he might say no.

"She's got a daughter about my age who already helps her out," I said. "She's got a treatment room in the house with all sorts of cool stuff and sick animals and everything."

"Bad enough we had to sell the farmhouse, and

now this lady is passing out jobs to kids. Who does she think she is, anyway?" Dad growled.

I looked at Steve, but he was pretending to still be very busy with the eggs he had already finished cooking.

"She's going to pay me," I said. "Only a few bucks an hour, but I don't care. I just want to be around the animals." I was careful not to say what kind of animals. I looked up at Dad, thinking, *Please don't say no, please don't say no.*

Dad didn't say anything for a full minute, just sat there looking red in the face.

"I started helping Poppaw chop tobacco when I was eight," Steve said. I shot him a grateful look. "I didn't want to, but he said a little hard work never hurt anybody. Even knucklehead here can't screw up cleaning out a cage or filling a water dish."

"Humph. Guess you're right about that," Dad said. "You really want to do this?"

"Yes, sir, I really do." I nodded and gave him my

best good-boy face. Dad leaned back and shook his head, looking at Steve, not me.

"All right, then, after you finish the dishes, we'll go talk to this lady vet of yours."

I could have hugged him, but Harper men aren't big on hugs. We are big on breakfast, so we went back to eating. Maybe I'd take a treat for the unicorn. Since she resembled a horse, she'd probably like apples or carrots, like horses do. I'd heard of feeding horses lumps of sugar, but we didn't buy sugar cubes, just bags. I could get some cubes when I got paid.

I mopped up the egg yolk with the last bit of toast, then carried my dishes to the sink. That's one of my main chores, washing dishes, ever since the dishwasher broke and flooded the kitchen.

It felt weird to go to the front door of the farmhouse. We always used to go through the kitchen door in the back.

Some of Grandma's rosebushes had been moved to the far side of the steps to make room for a new ramp going up to the porch. Some of the roses still had blooms—big red, pink, and white ones and two little peachy-yellow ones. Roses were her favorite flower, so I was glad to see they were still there. There was a bench under the living room window and a big sign next to the door that said BRANCUSI ANIMAL CLINIC. OFFICE HOURS 10 A.M.–4 P.M. Dad lingered a bit at the door, checking out the new paint job and the pots of flowers hanging all around. The door swung open to the sound of a jangling bell. A lady staggered out carrying a fat cocker spaniel with a plastic cone around its head, like some weird sort of shield against outer-space death rays. The dog's rump was shaved and looked coated with brown stain. We shuffled back to give them some room.

"Whoops!" cried the lady. "Excuse us, got to get my baby back home." The dog wagged its stumpy little tail and squirmed to get down. Dad held the screen door until they were safely past, then motioned for me to go on in.

The living room sure had changed. The carpets were gone and now the floors were just bare wood. Instead of easy chairs and a couch, there were plastic chairs and two wooden benches to sit on. A birdcage holding a rumpled parakeet rested on one of the benches next to an old man. The house smelled funny, too, like wet dogs and Clorox.

We sat on the other bench in front of the window. Dad pulled a Salem out of his shirt pocket. He flipped out his lighter, holding the flame to the end of the cigarette and drawing in the smoke. A flick of his wrist flipped the top back on the lighter; then he tucked it into his pocket. It was a Zippo that had belonged to Poppaw. The old man with the bird gave us a mean look.

"Dad," I whispered. "I don't think you're supposed to smoke in here."

"I don't see any No Smoking sign," he said.

"I don't see any ashtrays, either," I pointed out. "Besides, those things are bad for you." He gave me one of those looks, so I shut up. We waited for a while, Dad cupping the cigarette in his left hand, like a big wind might come along and blow it out. The old man kept giving us the evil eye, but Dad ignored him and kept smoking.

Chinaberry Creek is a small town and never had a vet before. Most folks had to go over to Concord

or Charlotte to get their animals treated. I wondered how much work there would really be for me to do.

Allegra came busting in through the dining room door, yelling, "No smoking in the clinic!" She thrust a trash can in Dad's face, then caught sight of me. "Oh, it's you," she said. "I'm sorry, but you can't smoke in here. It's bad for the patients."

Dad studied her for a second, then tossed the cigarette into the can. He crossed his arms and waited. Allegra looked flustered.

I jumped in to explain. "Dad, this is Allegra Brancusi, the girl I told you about." This was not off to a good start.

Dr. Brancusi walked up. "You must be Eric's father," she said, smiling and holding out her hand.

Dad stood up and said, "Yes, ma'am." He didn't shake her hand though. She looked a bit flustered too, and I could see how Allegra favored her.

"Come back into the kitchen and we'll talk. Allegra, why don't you take Eric out to the barn?"

Dad shot me his "you better behave yourself if you know what's good for you" look. I gave him my best smile and followed Allegra outside.

"Hey, wait up," I called. She had already rounded the side of the house before I got off the porch. There was a new fence with a gate across the driveway and a sign that said PRIVATE, DO NOT ENTER. The Brancusis sure were fond of signs. I hopped over the fence and caught up to Allegra at the barn door. "How's the unicorn doing?"

"Shhh!" Allegra hissed. "Don't talk about her outside; someone might hear you."

"Who, the squirrels?" I snorted. She slid the door open and jerked me inside. There was a big pile of wood shavings in the first stall. It was taller than my head. The other stalls were empty — no unicorn.

"Here." Allegra tossed a shovel at me. "You can start by mucking out the stall. Put it in the wheelbarrow and then dump it on the manure pile at the far side of the paddock."

"What?" I said.

"Muck out the stall. You know, scoop up the dirty bedding," she said, forcing the shovel into my hand. "Like cleaning a cat's box."

Suddenly, I got the picture. It wasn't pretty.

"You want me to pick up unicorn poop?" I asked, just to make sure.

"Well, duh," she said. She rolled a wheelbarrow out of a corner and parked it in front of the middle stall. "The stall has to be cleaned twice a day. Basic hygiene is the foundation of the practice of medicine," she went on. "Just wait until we have to sterilize a space."

When I had watched Allegra help her mother doctor the unicorn, I thought maybe she wasn't so bad after all. Wrong.

I trudged over to the unicorn's stall. Next to the wall was a big pile of dark brown lumps and a little farther back a wet clump of wood shavings. A sour stink came from the bedding, nothing like the flow-ery unicorn smell from the night before. That's all there was to see, a smelly bunch of unicorn poop.

"Where is she?" I demanded. My throat tightened with disappointment. I felt tricked, like the time Larry Aycock switched lunch bags and stuck me with his nasty old livermush sandwich. They didn't need my help; they just wanted a pooper-scooper.

"Probably down by the creek," Allegra replied. "She can bear some weight on that hoof now that the iron's been removed. The exercise will be good for her."

"But you said she needed to be watched," I cried. "Maybe she got worse, maybe she's in trouble. How do you know she'll come back?"

"Because she promised," said a rumbly voice from around my ankles. Something brushed along my leg, like a cat does when it wants to be fed. I looked down. It *was* a cat. Its little white head rubbed across my shins, while its long white tail stood up with the tip flopped over, making a little flag shape in the air. The face tilted up to catch my eyes.

"Unicorns are very noble, you know," the cat said. Then it winked at me.

CHAPTER FOUR

SUDDENLY, I NEEDED TO SIT DOWN. Actually I fell back flat on my butt, dropping the shovel with a clang. It wasn't just that the cat talked to me. I mean, I had touched a unicorn, so I knew there were magical creatures around. But it wasn't a complete cat. It had a head and a tail and nothing in between holding the parts together.

"Timothy!" scolded Allegra. "I told you to wait until I had a chance to tell Eric about you." She crouched down, touching my shoulder. "Are you all right?"

I nodded, still staring at the cat head. "Where's the rest of him?" I asked.

The head came closer and I felt little paws marching up my left leg.

"The rest of me is right here," Timothy said. "Just invisible." The head stopped, and the tail made a big white C shape across my lap. It felt like a cat was snuggling down; it just didn't look like it. With one finger, I reached behind the head and felt warm, soft fur and the string of bumps of his backbone underneath.

"Invisible," I said. "And you talk."

"I," the cat announced, "am a Cheshire cat." As if that explained everything.

"What's a Cheshire cat?" The cat's head lifted up and back and he stared down his nose. I think he sniffed at me, too.

"You know," Allegra said. "Like the cat in *Alice in Wonderland*. The one that talks to her and slowly turns invisible."

I looked at the white head in my lap, still glaring at me, and the white tail waving at the tip. "In the movie that cat was striped."

"Cheshire cats are not defined by something as ordinary as coloring," the cat informed me. "To be a Cheshire cat, one must have the ability to speak human language and to become invisible at will. True Cheshire cats are quite rare." Dipping his head, he stuck out his tongue and waved it in the air. Then his right ear folded down and popped back up. I realized he must be washing himself—licking his invisible paw and then using it to brush his ear.

"Cool!" I said. "Why don't you turn back visible now? Or all invisible? Ow, what was that for?" Little bunches of claws needled my leg as he turned around. His tail was raised high in the air, precisely in the center between his ears as he stalked away, tail tip lashing. Can you say something walked when you can't see its legs?

"Oh, dear," Allegra said. "Timothy, come back. Eric doesn't know." The head and tail kept going. "Timothy can't control his visibility anymore. He's stuck that way. It's very embarrassing to him. That's why he's here. We're trying to figure out how to help. Mom thinks it might have started with some sort of allergic reaction." She stood up and craned her neck, looking for him. "Timothy!" she called again. No answer.

I stood too. "He still has a body, right?" I could feel the effect of his claws, and his weight on my lap.

"Right, the invisibility only affects what you can see, it doesn't make him intangible. He says he can't see his invisible parts either."

I pondered this for a bit. Seemed like it wouldn't matter that much, not seeing your body, as long as everything worked all right. But it would be hard to put a Band-Aid on a banged-up knee if you couldn't see it. Going out in public would be tricky; people would definitely stare.

"Timothy was our first supernatural exotic patient. It bugs Mom that she hasn't been able to cure him, although she did clear up his infestation of ear mites. He is safer here with us as long as he's only partly visible. And he likes having such a big territory to roam around in." Allegra handed me the shovel again. "Well, back to work. After mucking out the stall, mop the floor with this disinfectant, then put down about six inches of fresh bedding." She handed me a bucket and started toward the door.

"Hey, aren't you going to help me?" I asked.

"Nope," she said, giving a little wave as she walked out into the sunlight.

So I started my new job, scooping up unicorn poop. Holding my breath, I slid the flat of the shovel under the pile of lumps. Only one lump fell off as I took the stuff over to the wheelbarrow. Scooped that up too. After a couple of minutes, the wheelbarrow was full. I rolled it outside and found the beginning of the manure pile across the yard, past the edge of the fence.

The fence was new, made out of planks covered with chicken wire. They must have added it as a safe place for the animals to run around while they recovered. The manure pile was new too, but it had already attracted a bunch of big black flies. A couple decided that I made a nice snack, a little dessert after the main course of fresh-tossed manure. Big red welts popped up on my arms.

I mopped and then spread a new layer of bedding. It didn't smell so bad now, or maybe I was just getting used to it. I wasn't sure where the shovel was supposed to go, so I propped it next to the stall door.

The barn door slid open. "I've turned this into our treatment area for large animals," Dr. Brancusi was explaining to my dad as they stepped inside. Allegra was trailing behind them. "My practice is mostly small animals, but sometimes I do get livestock to treat." Dad was taking it all in, all the changes to the barn, nodding and making polite "uh-huh" sounds. Then he focused on me.

"How'd you get wood chips all over you?"

Dr. Brancusi laughed. "That's my fault," she said. "We had a horse here last night and I had Allegra show Eric how to clean out the stall. I'm afraid he might come home covered in wood chips pretty often."

Dad gave a little "humph," like he knew I'd come home filthy no matter what. "The doctor and me, we have an understanding about your work here, so I'm going back home. You work hard and do what the lady tells you."

"Yes, sir," I said. He scanned the barn again, the wood chips, the new white paint on the walls and trim, and back at me. I thought he might say something more, but he just pointed a finger at me, then turned and left.

Dr. Brancusi was looking as if she didn't know quite what to do with me now. Allegra was quiet for once. "I'm going to bring the unicorn back in," Dr. Brancusi said. "Why don't you two fix her some water and feed?" She went out the back door of the barn and into the woods.

After a few minutes, the doctor came back, the

unicorn following behind. The unicorn still hobbled a bit, favoring the bandaged foot. She was even more beautiful than she had seemed last night; the sunlight made her coat glow a creamy white, and her mane was lit like spun sugar.

When she reached the door, I swear she recognized me. She dipped her head like a greeting. "Open the stall, doofus," said Allegra, elbowing me. I swung the door open and the unicorn stepped in like a queen coming home. That rose and pine smell lifted off her, and I couldn't resist stroking her back as she passed. She turned and then nudged my hand with her nose.

"Hey, pretty girl," I said, rubbing that velvety face. "Are you feeling better, sweetie?" I didn't even care that Allegra heard me baby-talking the unicorn, I was so glad to see her again. "Where was she?" I asked.

"I thought your dad might want to see the barn, so I took her to a fenced-in yard I had built in that little meadow over the hill. We need a private place to exercise some of our more unusual patients," Dr. Brancusi said.

Allegra came up on her other side and began stroking the unicorn's neck. "There's a good girl," Allegra cooed. "How's my Lady Shimmershine Moonpearl?"

"Shimmershine Moonpearl?"

"She needed a name, so I gave her one. She likes it, don't you, Lady Shimmershine Moonpearl," Allegra said. "It's so elegant, just like she is."

I thought it was the dumbest thing I'd ever heard. The unicorn snorted a bit and shook her mane. She did need a name, but a better one than that. I looked at the swirling horn. Grandma had some pearls that were that kind of soft white color. Pearl wouldn't be so bad. Allegra was scratching the unicorn's ears, and they both looked happy.

"It's kind of long," I said. "How about Pearl for short?"

"Pearl is so ordinary," Allegra said. "Moonpearl is better." She had a point. The unicorn did deserve a special name.

"OK. Moonpearl," I said. Allegra smiled at me.

Dr. Brancusi came into the stall, carrying the med kit. "Time to change her dressing. Eric, keep petting her while we work." Allegra assisted, just like before. This was more like it, helping this beautiful creature, holding her soft muzzle, looking into her acorn-green eye.

"Hey, Moonpearl," I whispered. Dr. Brancusi looked up at me.

"We named her," said Allegra. "Lady Shimmershine Moonpearl — Moonpearl for short."

"Nice name," the doctor said. She stood up and moved so the unicorn could see her, speaking directly to Moonpearl. "I am going to hold off on the antibiotics, but I need to change the dressing a couple of times a day. If the infection is still lingering tomorrow, you will need three days of shots. Understand?"

Moonpearl nodded her head and reached to nuzzle the doctor too. "Terrific. You're a good patient." She patted the unicorn's neck. Allegra was stroking her sides. I don't know how long we all stood there, petting the unicorn.

"Does she purr?" a small growly voice said. "*I* purr when someone bothers to pet me." Timothy's head and straight-up tail came bobbing into the stall.

Dr. Brancusi laughed and scooped up the cat. She scratched him behind the ears and he purred, his eyes half-closed, just like any old barn cat. "Silly boy, we still love you," she said. It gave me a shiver to see that little white head and tail floating around, not connected to anything.

Moonpearl huffed and turned to look at Timothy. He looked back, ears twitching, eyes wide. The cat's head twisted around, and the doctor opened her arms. Then he was on the ground, staring up at the unicorn.

Moonpearl nickered low, tapped her hoof a couple of times, and shook her head at Dr. Brancusi.

"I shall tell her that," Timothy said.

"Do you speak her language?" asked the doctor.

"Not precisely," said Timothy, "but we can communicate after a fashion. She does understand English, and probably most other human languages. We magical creatures have a type of *lingua franca*, mostly signs and gestures that we use amongst ourselves. As I told you last night, she promised to come back, and so she did."

"What did she say just now?" Allegra wanted to know. Of course, I was wondering too.

"She says that twins are not uncommon among unicorns, but that babies born during the cold moons often don't survive. She wants to stay here, so her babies will live," he told us.

"I will help you all that I can, but I can't promise to save them. You will need to let me examine you frequently and let me treat you," Dr. Brancusi said. She looked down at Timothy. "Does she understand?" she asked the cat.

Moonpearl snorted and flicked her ears.

"She agrees to your terms," he said.

With a little huff, the unicorn stepped forward, looming over Timothy, or at least over his head.

"Really?" the cat said. "A most generous offer, my lady."

"Now what did she say?" Allegra asked.

"She offered to touch me with her horn."

"So?" I said.

"So," Timothy said, "unicorns have powers of healing. You felt it. It's why you were all standing there like ninnies with silly smiles on your faces. Just seeing a unicorn can lift your spirits. But the greatest power is concentrated in the horn."

The cat's head and tail were floating in a small circle in front of the unicorn. I guess he was pacing back and forth, the way cats do when they see something they want out the window, but can't get to it.

"Do you think she can cure you?" Dr. Brancusi asked. "Is there any risk involved, to you or her?"

"I'm not sure," Timothy said. "Certainly not to me, but sometimes using magical power has a cost."

The doctor moved out to the side where the unicorn could see her better. Her face was serious. "Don't do this if it will weaken you. You still have an infection that could develop complications. Understood?"

The unicorn snorted and nodded her head. I swear it looked like she rolled her eyes, as if she were saying, "Yeah, yeah, whatever." Allegra was trying not to smile, so I think she saw it too.

"She understands," Timothy said. "I accept your help, my lady."

His head stopped a few inches below her muzzle. He closed his eyes, the end of his tail twitching. The unicorn backed up a few steps, curved her neck, and lowered her head. Light seemed to slip down the spiral of the horn. Gently, she brushed Timothy, just once, between his ears with the tip of her horn.

For a moment, nothing seemed to happen. There was no flash, explosion, or strange smell. There was a tension in the air, like a low humming or that feeling just before a thunderstorm when you know that there will be lightning. Timothy didn't move. Then the air between his head and tail got misty. The mist grew thicker. I could see a cat-shape coming into focus, a sleek body and four legs placed squarely beneath. Timothy kept his eyes closed tight. The shape grew firmer. I could see the hairs of his fur coat. At last, there stood an ordinary cat — head and tail attached to a body with a black splotch on the back and black front legs and white paws.

I looked up at Allegra and her mom. This was awesome. We were all grinning like fools.

"Well," Timothy demanded. "Did it work?" His eyes were squinched shut.

"See for yourself," said Dr. Brancusi.

The cat opened his eyes and looked down. He laughed and plopped onto his back, waving his legs in the air. I'd never heard a cat laugh. It was kind of rumbly, like a purr. "There you are, my beauties," he cooed. "All toes present and accounted for. Oh, happiness!" Allegra and her mom were both grinning at him and at me, until I had to laugh too.

Sprawling on the ground, Timothy stretched, reaching out one rear leg, then the other. Rolling up to his feet, he craned his neck to inspect his back. "But my fur is in a shocking state. One just can't groom properly when partially invisible." He gave his belly a few licks, then jumped up and darted over to the unicorn.

"Many thanks, my lady," Timothy said, making a funny little bow by folding his front legs. The unicorn nickered in return. Maybe it was her version of a laugh. Timothy settled in a corner of the stall for a serious session of grooming.

CHAPTER FIVE

THE NEXT MORNING, I STOPPED by my treehouse on the way to the clinic. I used a couple of thumbtacks to fasten a No Trepassing sign to the trunk. Now that I knew why Allegra had posted the property, I figured it couldn't hurt to have one on my tree. It was a good spot and easy to see on that side of the ridge. I didn't think she would notice that I used one from another, less visible tree.

As usual for Sundays, Dad and Steve were sleeping in. I was used to getting up by myself to go to church with Grandma, until she went into the nursing home. They probably wouldn't think any-thing about my being gone.

I checked the barn first, but the doors were locked and the paddock was empty. I went around to the front door and knocked. Nothing. I couldn't see through the curtains, but it didn't look like any lights were on. I went into the front yard, checking out the windows, but couldn't see anything there either. Maybe they were having breakfast in the kitchen. A huge new washer and dryer sat right next to the door on the screened-in back porch. A little frilly curtain covered the kitchen door window. I knocked and waited. The curtain moved aside and I saw a gray-haired lady holding a big knife. I jumped back. *Who was that?* She smiled and disappeared for a moment, then opened the door.

"You must be Eric," she said. "Come in, come in." She waved the knife around, but not in my general direction, so I did what she said. The kitchen was changed too. Everything was new, white cabinets and lots more lights. Instead of the red-trimmed metal table and chairs, there was a kitchen island in the middle of the room, covered with a big pile of chopped meat and a bunch of dishes filled with mushy brown stuff. There were stacks of dishes and bowls around the sink and in big plastic bins, soaking in dark blue water.

"Kris told me about you," she said. "I'm Georgia McIntyre, but you can call me Georgie. Everybody does." She pointed to herself with the knife. "I'm the office manager and vet tech. Pardon me if I don't shake hands, but I'm in the midst of fixing the meals here. Hygiene, you know." Her other hand waved a dishrag toward the pile of meat. Maybe she was making a stew, but that brown mush didn't look too good.

"Yes, ma'am," I said, just to be on the safe side.

She scooped the chopped meat into a plastic bowl and stuck it in the fridge. "I'll just finish up these before I show you where the mop is, unless you'd rather learn the kitchen protocol first."

Mop? Kitchen protocol? I thought. Oh, man, working in here was going to be just as bad as working in the barn. I didn't cook too much at home, just sandwiches mostly, although Steve was getting to be a pretty good cook now that he worked at the diner. How hard could it be to fix feed for some animals? The lady put lids on a few more things and put them away.

"It shouldn't take you long. We don't have many boarders this weekend, so the floor isn't too bad," Georgie said, pulling a broom out of the pantry closet. She handed it to me along with a dustpan. "Sweep in the waiting room first, then the rest of the downstairs rooms. Don't worry about the surgery for now. Kris and Allegra should be back from mass shortly." She made little shooing motions with her hands, so I went down the hall into what used to be my grandma's living room and swept the floor. That was easy enough, except for a few bits of fur that kept floating off the dustpan when I tried to empty it. The dining room was an office now, with two desks and a bunch of file cabinets where the china hutch used to sit. The spare bedroom, where I used to stay, had been made into two small rooms, each with a steel table in the middle and a couple of cafeteria-type chairs. I kind of missed the little brass bed I slept in; I should have asked to keep it when they cleared out the house. But then I would've had to give up the bed that my mom had picked out.

I opened the door to the room that used to be Grandma's bedroom. It had shelves full of cages and aquariums with screened tops. It smelled like wet dog and something strong and sharp and damp. A couple of the aquariums had a layer of wood shavings and a card clipped to the side. In one, a white rat was curled up in the corner. There was a sorry-looking mutt with his hind leg in a cast, sleeping on his side, in a cage on a bottom shelf. I'd just finished sweeping when Allegra came in, pushing one of those big yellow buckets on wheels like the school janitors use.

"Here," she whispered, motioning me over. She lifted the mop and dropped the head into the wringer attached to the bucket. She squeezed out the water, careful not to get any on her dress, and shoved the mop handle at me. "Try not to make too much noise," she said, still whispering.

"Why not?" I asked, in my normal voice.

"You'll stress the patients," she answered, gesturing to the cages. "Strange voices can frighten them."

"They all must be scared when they hear you," I whispered back.

The mutt lifted his head and whimpered a bit. Allegra cut her eyes at me, then went over to his cage, making little cooing sounds. He thumped his tail.

While I mopped, she took the water bowls and dishes out of the mutt's cage and the aquariums. She set them on a tray on the table by the window.

"Bring those into the kitchen when you've finished mopping," she whispered and left. Didn't even look back to see if I'd nodded in agreement or anything. When I finished, I picked up the tray. I noticed a big jar holding some scummy-looking water with bubbles along the sides. It smelled bad, so I took that too.

Back in the kitchen, Georgie was putting things away. "Those go on the left side of the sink," she said. "Dirty dishes on the left, clean and sterile dishes on the right. You can scrape the food into this trash can."

I plunked down the tray and tossed bits of dried-up fruit and brown mess into the trash. I picked up the jar to pour the nasty water down the sink.

"Stop!" cried Georgie. I nearly dropped the jar. "Don't pour that out, that's a squonk!"

"A what?"

"A squonk. It's a patient, not trash." Georgie took

the jar away from me. "Oh, dear, it had been looking so promising, too."

"What's a squonk?" I asked.

"Squonks are very shy creatures, ashamed of their appearance. Imagine a cross between a duck-billed platypus and a toad, with slimy skin and lots of warts. They cry constantly because of their ugliness. When captured, they dissolve into tears to avoid being seen." She draped a dishtowel across a countertop and gently set down the jar.

The water was quivering in an odd fashion, with a swirl in the center like a blob of brownish jellyfish.

Tiny bubbles rose to the surface and popped, releasing a rotten egg smell. "How do you know what it looks like?" I asked.

"Kris said this one is very bold for its kind. When we leave it alone long enough, it solidifies again, so I've caught a few glimpses. Sometimes it sings, so we know it's doing well. They usually don't range this far south. Squonks are a breed of 'fearsome critters' that Paul Bunyan's lumberjacks discovered." Georgie leaned over the jar. "There, there, pretty; it's just Eric."

"Paul Bunyan?" I said. "He's not real. He's just a character in stories."

"So are unicorns, but that creature out in the barn is just as real as you are, and so is this squonk." She picked up the jar, taking pains to carry it level so the water wouldn't slosh too much, when Allegra and Dr. Brancusi came in.

"What's the squonk doing in here?" Allegra demanded.

"Just a little misunderstanding," Georgie said. "Eric thought the jar needed cleaning. I'll put this back where it belongs."

"Cleaning?" Allegra screeched. "Did he hurt it?" She whirled around to glare at me as Georgie slipped past her with the jar. "Mom, I told you this was a bad idea. He doesn't know anything; he's going to mess things up."

"How was I supposed to know that stinky water was a — a creature?" I said. "It doesn't look any different from the mop water. Nobody told me about it and it was next to all those other dirty dishes. I wouldn't hurt anything on purpose." It wasn't fair. All I really wanted to do was hang out with Moonpearl, and all I did was clean up stinky messes.

"Allegra," Dr. Brancusi said, "he couldn't have known." Allegra pouted, her mouth all scrunched up. The doctor sighed, then turned to me. "We haven't had any new help in a long time. I'm afraid we're not doing a very good job of training you."

I blinked at that. I wasn't used to grownups apologizing to me. "It's OK," I said.

"Why don't you go out to the barn and muck out the stall. The unicorn is in the paddock. I'll be out in a bit and show you how to curry her and what to feed her," she said. I didn't need to be told that twice, so I left.

Mucking out the stall wasn't so bad this time. It didn't stink as much as that squonk. As I pushed the loaded wheelbarrow over to the compost pile, the unicorn came trotting over to me.

"Hey, beauty, hey, Moonpearl," I said as she stopped a few feet away. I stretched out my hand and waited. She stepped closer and nuzzled my fingers with her nose. It was so soft, like the skin of a ripe peach. Slowly, I turned my hand over and rubbed between her nostrils. The little whiskers on the end tickled. "Hey, darling, you like me, don't you?" I whispered to her, real low. I slowly ran my hand along her nose to the base of the horn, but I didn't touch it. Her ears flicked and I drew my hand back.

"She doesn't want you to touch that," a voice rumbled. Something brushed my leg. It was that cat, Timothy. The unicorn took a step back and nudged the cat's side with her nose.

"I didn't."

"Good," said Timothy. He rubbed up against my leg again. "It's a thing of power, that horn. Not to be trifled with." He sat down and began cleaning his fur. "She likes you, you know."

"Really?" Pleased, I looked at Moonpearl, who rubbed her muzzle against my arm.

"Can't see why." Timothy sniffed. "You're just an ordinary boy."

"Not that ordinary," said the doctor, walking up with a bucket full of brushes. "He's coped pretty well with all the strangeness we've thrown at him." She set the bucket down next to me. "Here, let me show you how to groom a unicorn. I've done it twice now, so that makes me an expert, I guess. They didn't cover this in vet school, but she seemed to like it." The doctor pulled a couple of brushes out of the bucket and handed me one. I slipped my hand under the strap on the back just like she did.

"This is a curry comb. Use it like this on her neck and body." She started just below the unicorn's head, rubbing the comb in little circles. "It loosens the dirt, so we can wipe it off easily. Don't use it on her legs, I have something else for that." I stretched out my hand and rubbed the comb lightly on Moonpearl's white shoulder. She made a soft huffing sound. The doctor went around the unicorn's head and began working on the other side. "Tell me if you see any sores or scratches on her skin, anything that looks unhealthy."

I nodded and moved the comb along her sides. This was all I wanted, to be taking care of this beauty.

She felt smooth and strong beneath the comb, that smell of earth and roses and pine rising from her skin.

"This will be one of your regular tasks, Eric," said Dr. Brancusi. "After mucking out the stall and seeing that she has enough water and feed, you should groom her each day."

"Really?" I said. "Thanks, ma'am."

"No need to be so formal. You can call me Kris."

I wasn't sure about that; it didn't seem right. Grandma always insisted I mind my manners. Dr. Brancusi noticed I wasn't too comfortable with her suggestion and said, "Or how about Dr. B."

"Dr. B., that's good."

I was working my way to the back of the unicorn when I noticed her tail. It wasn't long and flowing, like a horse tail or a girl's ponytail. It was more like a lion's tail, covered with fur, with a big tuft of long hair on the end. The tail was white, but the tuft was darker. I hadn't really paid attention to it before; I just thought her tail would be like a regular horse's. Dr. B. saw what I was looking at and gave a little laugh.

"It surprised me a bit too, but she's not really a horse. We'll use a different brush for the tail and a comb on the tuft," she said.

"Poor sort of creature that needs so much help cleaning herself," said Timothy. "But then, we can't all be cats." He stuck his hind leg in the air and licked it, making a circle of himself. I laughed and the cat glared at me. He was almost as bad as Allegra for giving me the stink eye.

Dr. B. taught me how to use a body brush and how to comb out the unicorn's mane and tail tuft, and then wipe down her legs and face with a soft cloth. We changed the bandage on the hurt hoof, and I got to prepare the gauze and ointment this time.

Next, Dr. B. showed me where she kept the feed and where the new water spigot was. We hadn't needed running water when the barn was used as a garage. The unicorn seemed hungry and I wished I'd remembered to bring her a carrot or an apple.

"It's about lunchtime for people, too. Would you like to join us?" asked Dr. B.

Lunchtime? I didn't know it was that late.

"No thank you, ma'am, I mean, Dr. B. I'm expected home." I left the barn, but said over my shoulder, "I'll be back tomorrow, right after school. Gotta go." I ran for home, hoping Dad hadn't missed me yet.

CHAPTER SIX

I RACED UP THE RIDGE, stopping to catch my breath at the top. Dad's car was still in the driveway, so maybe I was back in time. I ran down to the house. Just as I reached for the screen door to the kitchen, Steve opened it. "Where've you been, dweeb?"

"Working."

"Oh, yeah, the animal thing. Might want to change your clothes," he said.

I looked down. There were wood shavings all over my shirt, and more stuff on my shoes. I just had time to change my shoes when Dad hollered for me to hurry.

I knocked straw and shavings off my pant leg as I went down the steps. Dad and Steve were already buckled in, so I slipped into the back seat.

"You're late," Dad said, looking at me in the rear-view mirror. Why did everybody have to cut their eyes at me? He didn't sound too mad, though.

"Sorry." I slumped back in the seat. Steve fiddled with the radio, and nobody said anything more. We got there about eleven forty-five, not too much later than our usual eleven thirty. Nothing ever changes at the Three Oaks Nursing Home. The same two old men were sitting in chairs by the front door, nodding at everybody who came in. When we walked into the lobby, it struck me how it smelled like the animal clinic — strong and sharp, like bleach and pee.

Mrs. Wheeler came rolling up. "Have you seen my Betty? She's coming to take me home today." Dad had told me that her Betty died twenty years ago. I wasn't sure which was sadder, that she didn't remember or that she was always disappointed because Betty never came.

Grandma was lying in bed, her hair all scraggly on her pillow. She still had that IV pole with the bag of stuff hanging from it. She must have been doing better though, because she was wearing her Sunday clothes. I couldn't get used to how tiny she looked in the bed. Maybe it was the rails on each side, like a little kid's bed.

We tried to be quiet because she looked to be asleep, but she smiled without opening her eyes and said, "I hear my boys." Dad leaned over and kissed her forehead.

"Hey, Mama," he said. "I brought your magazines." All her magazines and mail have been coming to our house since she moved to Three Oaks. He plopped down in a chair next to the bed.

"Set them on the dresser; I'll look at them later,"

she said, opening her eyes and waving her curled-up hand to the side. She held out her arms. "Come on, now, where are the rest of my kisses?" Steve gave her a quick peck on the cheek and took up his place in the chair by the window.

I gave my kiss next, but I let her hug me, too, sitting on the bed with her. Hugging Grandma used to be like being wrapped in a blanket, folded in safe. She was still soft, but she didn't feel so big anymore. She took a deep breath, sniffing my hair, and let out a long sigh.

"You smell like the woods," she said, hugging me tighter. "I'd almost forgotten what a good smell that is." She let go and I sat back up. She pulled herself up a little straighter in the bed too, petting my arm, her eyes bright. "I do miss being in our woods."

Dad was clicking through the channels on the TV and Steve was watching as he looked for the game with their favorite teams, so they didn't especially notice what happened next. Grandma pulled a long white hair off my shirt sleeve—a unicorn hair, probably from Moonpearl's mane.

"What have you been playing with, Eric?" she asked. "This is too long to be dog hair. Looks more like a horse hair."

"Yeah, I've got a job, helping that lady vet who bought your house. Um, there's a horse staying in the barn now that I'm helping take care of." As I told Grandma about the clinic, she found another hair on my pant leg, and a third on my shirt front. I had lots of white hairs clinging to my clothes. I tried brushing them off, but then they stuck to the bedcovers.

Raising her hands to her face, Grandma took a deep breath. Then she stretched out her fingers and spread them flat, the unicorn hairs lying in the middle of her hand. That hand had been all twisted up since forever because of arthritis, and that first finger was so crooked she could barely move it. Open and close, open and close, her fingers moved slow and smooth. The fingers were still crooked, but they moved.

"All right!" shouted Steve, pumping the air with his fists. "Did you see that?" At first I thought he meant Grandma's hand, but he was looking at the TV, not at us.

"Right into the stands," said Dad. "Sweet."

"Those two would rather watch baseball than eat," said Grandma, smiling a bit as she watched them. Steve flashed her a grin and then turned back to the game. Well, it was the beginning of the World Series. Grandma looked at me, then carefully brushed the unicorn hairs into a little dish on her bedside table that held bobby pins and safety pins. "I'll just keep these," she whispered, "to remind me of my favorite blue-eyed grandbaby." She'd called me that since I was little. My eyes were blue, but Steve's were brown. I picked another hair off my pant leg and added it to the pile. She patted my hand.

"Speaking of eating, I do believe it's dinnertime," Grandma said in a loud voice. "Jimmy, help your old mother into her chair."

"Sure, Mama," said Dad, coming around to the side of the bed. He helped her with the covers and eased her feet over the side. I hopped off the bed and rolled the wheelchair out of the corner. I was excited. Grandma hadn't been out of bed when we were there in a long time; she usually said she was too tired.

I positioned the wheelchair next to the bed. She put her hands around Dad's neck and he leaned back, lifting her off the bed and swinging her toward the chair. One leg was still sort of twisted up from when she had that stroke. I scooted the wheelchair up under her and she settled down into the seat. She motioned for her hairbrush. I handed it to her and she primped for a bit, swinging her right foot back and forth.

"OK, boys, let's roll!" Grandma cried. As Dad pushed the chair, Grandma waved to everybody in the hall on the way to the dining room. I pulled the IV pole alongside them, Steve shuffling behind us.

We found a table where we could all sit together. Dad and Grandma started talking about a whole bunch of people from her church who I didn't know. She was using her right hand to eat with again.

This set me to thinking. I had never heard of unicorn hair being magic. Of course, I hadn't heard much about unicorns, period, except for the one-horn business, so what did I know?

Steve nudged my foot with his under the table. "Check it out," he whispered, nodding in the direction of the girl bringing the tray.

"You already have a girlfriend," I said.

"So? Doesn't hurt to look." He leaned back so the girl could set down the tray. "Thank you, miss," he said. She seemed a bit surprised, but kept on taking the plates off the tray and arranging them in front of Grandma.

"Stevie, quit distracting the girl," Grandma said. "He's a good boy, just a bit full of himself," she said. The girl asked if we needed anything, then left.

Grandma gave me her dinner roll. I munched down on it, still wondering about the unicorn hair. If three little unicorn hairs made her hand so much better, maybe Moonpearl could make her all better, well enough to come home. I guessed not to her home, because Dr. B. probably wouldn't sell the farmhouse back to us. We couldn't afford to change it back to the way it was even if she did. But I'd give up my room and move in with Steve if it meant that Grandma could live with us and not in this place.

CHAPTER SEVEN

THAT MONDAY WAS THE FIRST school day since I'd started working at the Brancusi Animal Clinic. Dr. B. didn't expect me until late in the afternoon, so when I got off the bus, I was surprised to see Timothy trotting down the driveway. He stopped a few feet away and craned his neck around, scanning the area. I looked too, but didn't see anything unusual, at least not more unusual than a Cheshire cat.

"Hurry up, boy," Timothy said. "They need your help." Before I could answer, he took off across the yard. I dumped my backpack on the front porch and ran after him. Timothy was nowhere to be seen when I stopped on the clinic's kitchen steps to catch my breath.

Allegra came bombing out of the door. "It's about time you got here. I've been home for half an hour."

"Hello to you, too," I said, still puffing.

"Do you know where there's a pond or a creek around here?" she asked.

"Sure," I said, a bit surprised at the question. "There's a pond at the other end of the cow pasture, behind the ridge, and a creek not far beyond that, but it's all still Harper land."

"Great," said Allegra. "Take me there." She started walking toward the ridge, really fast, taking the path back to my house.

"Why?" I asked. "Hey, wait, not that way." I pointed to another path, not so clear, that went up the slope.

"Prissy has escaped. She does it a lot this time of year, and always finds water," Allegra said, over her shoulder. She didn't slow down, but went stomping straight up the hill. I ran to catch up.

"Who's Prissy?"

"Our goose."

"A goose?" I stopped running. "You got me running around like a crazy person for a goose?"

Allegra whirled around. "Yes, a goose. She's got a bad wing and can't fly, but she keeps trying. We have to find her before she gets hurt. Come on."

"Lord love a duck," I muttered. It was one of those things Grandma used to say when she thought someone was being a fool. I trudged up the hill, passing Allegra. "This way." We walked and skidded down the other side of the ridge. At the bottom was the cow pasture, marked off with a barbed-wire fence. I held down the lower strand with my foot and held the other one up for Allegra to step through. At least she had enough manners to say thanks as I followed.

The cow pond was on the other side of the pasture,

surrounded by trees and low scrub. The grass was pretty high, as nobody kept cows here anymore. Allegra charged on ahead. I caught up to her by the edge of the pond. The water was still—no sign of a goose.

"Why don't you go that way and I'll go this way. We'll meet on the other side," I suggested.

"Fine," said Allegra. "Here, Prissy, here Priss, Priss, Priss," she called.

I skirted the edge of the water, looking around the bushes for a goose, but no luck. Allegra came up to me.

"She's not here. Now what?"

"We'll look by the creek, over this way." I led her up another little rise and down to the creek. Timothy was sitting curled up on a rock in the sun at the edge of the stream.

"Have you seen Prissy?" Allegra asked.

Timothy opened one eye. "No." Then he closed it and rolled over, turning his back to us. We searched upstream for a while and then came down to where Timothy was still on his rock. I sat down on a bigger rock nearby. Allegra plopped down next to me.

"We need to find her before dark," she said.

I didn't say anything. I thought the stupid goose would find its way home when it was hungry. Then we heard something splashing.

"Prissy?"

There was a low honk from downstream. Allegra took off after the sound, shouting, "Prissy! Prissy, come home now!"

"I suppose we have to help," said Timothy. He uncurled and began trotting toward the noise.

Around the bend, there was Allegra, chasing after a big white goose that was paddling down the creek. Sure enough, one wing didn't fold back as pretty as the other, and as she got closer, I saw the bandage on it.

I picked my way over a couple of rocks to the other side, hoping to shoo the goose back to Allegra. She was talking to it, trying to coax it out of the creek. I came up behind the goose.

"Come here, Prissy," Allegra cooed. Suddenly, it reared back, flapping its wings and throwing water all around. It snaked its head down and hissed at me. I stopped, spreading out my arms to wave it toward Allegra. Then it charged up the bank, honking and hissing, flapping right at me. I back-pedaled and tripped, landing flat on my back. The goose fluttered up a few feet, then landed on my chest with a thump, knocking the wind out of me. I tried to push it off so I could breathe, but it was heavy. It hissed again and poked its beak right in my face, snapping at my nose! I threw my hands up and it nipped my little finger.

"Prissy, stop that," Allegra yelled. The goose hissed at me again, turning around on my stomach, lifting and placing one foot, then the other. It felt like getting punched. How could something that size hurt so much?

It circled one more time and poked its wet straggly

tail toward my face. Then it hunkered down and made a grunting noise. Something warm and wet pressed on my stomach. The goose gave a big honk and hopped off me to the side.

I looked down and saw that that goose had laid an egg on me. A big, fat, shiny, golden goose egg.

CHAPTER EIGHT

A GOLDEN EGG! THAT GOOSE laid a golden egg, right in my lap. It was dark gold and heavy. I touched it, real gentle. It was warm. The shell felt just like a regular chicken egg, smooth, but a little grainy at the same time.

"Give me that!" Allegra snatched the egg away. The goose hissed and flapped its wings.

"Hey! I wasn't going to hurt it," I said, throwing up my hand to keep off the goose. It—I guess it was really a she—hissed again, weaving her head around.

"You can't have it," Allegra said. "We need this

egg." She backed away from me. Huh, I bet she did. We could use that egg too — it must be worth about a gazillion dollars.

"She laid it in my lap, so seems like it should be part mine. Finders, keepers," I said, just to make her mad. It did. She hugged the egg tight and kicked at me.

"I knew it, I knew we shouldn't trust you!" She whirled around and started running up the path.

"That's not fair!" I yelled back. "I haven't told anybody anything!" I took off after her. That old goose hissed and snapped at me as I passed her. I caught up with Allegra near the top of the rise. "I don't want your old egg anyway."

"You can't have it!" she yelled. "These eggs help pay for the clinic, for taking care of the patients like Timothy and the unicorn."

I stopped still. Oh. I never thought about how much it cost. Medical stuff is expensive; I knew that. We had to sell the farmhouse to pay for Grandma's hospital bills, even before she went into the nursing home. Allegra kept running down the hill. Then that mean old goose nipped me on the leg.

"Oww!" I kicked at the nasty thing as it waddled by, chasing after Allegra and her egg. That's what I get for trying to help, bit and left behind. Allegra was almost at the cow pond, the goose honking after her. They were as mean as snakes, that girl and that goose, both of them. Allegra stopped at the pond, looking confused.

I thought about leaving them to find their own way back. Then I remembered the unicorn. Allegra might not let me see Moonpearl again if I did that, and Dr. B. might even agree with her. I ran down the hill to where she was standing. I touched her on the shoulder.

She whirled around and I saw she had been crying.

"Don't you see, you stupid *boy!* If you take the

egg, then people will find out about Prissy and all the other creatures and they'll take them away and lock them up," she said. "I wish Mom had never let you hang around. Who asked you to butt into our business, learning all our secrets?" Her face was all blotchy and she was crying harder.

"You're the stupid one," I yelled back. "You want me to keep your precious secrets but you treat me like, like I'm a toad or something. You'd probably be nicer to a toad than to me."

She wiped her eyes with her sleeve and I thought she might have smiled. "I probably would," she said, grudgingly. "Toads are cuter than you." That was better. I didn't care if she thought toads were cuter than me, as long as she quit crying.

"I won't tell anyone about the egg, I promise." I spit in my hand and held it out to her. "I'll shake on it, so you know I mean it."

"Ewww. No."

"Ewww? You're the one who had me shoveling unicorn poop." I dropped my hand. "I haven't told anyone about the unicorn, or Timothy either."

"It's only been four days. You have to keep this secret forever," she said. "You don't know how hard it can get. We've had Timothy for three years and he's easy, he understands not to talk and to keep out of sight when other people are around. But I can't have girlfriends sleep over at our house, because they might see something. Some days, I want to tell someone so bad, because it's just so great to catch a glimpse of the squonk or see a fire lizard fly again after Mom fixed his wing."

I hadn't thought about it that way before. It wasn't hard not to tell Steve; he would do something lame, like charge his friends five bucks to see the unicorn. I wished I could tell my grandma though. She would love Moonpearl, just like me. She'd love Timothy, too. She might even like the stupid goose, who had caught up with us again.

"Now you can tell me."

She sniffled a bit. "I guess." I started up the path to the farm.

"Wait," she called. I looked back. At least she had stopped crying. "Wipe your hand off." She stuck out her hand. I wiped mine on my jeans and took hers to shake.

"Promise you'll never tell about the magical animals. Cross your heart, hope to die, lose your eyes if you lie?" she asked, squeezing hard.

"I'll never tell. Cross my heart, hope to die, lose my eyes if I lie." I didn't see how this promise was

any stronger than a spit shake one, but I did it anyway. She looked at me hard for a couple seconds, then dropped my hand.

"OK," she said and smiled.

"OK."

"I'll take the egg to Mom. You can bring Prissy back to the barn, now that you understand why she can't stay out in the woods." She tossed this order over her shoulder as she walked away. "I'm trusting you."

I could see that having Allegra trust me didn't mean she was going to stop bossing me around. I looked down at the goose. The goose gave me an evil look.

"Honk," she said.

CHAPTER NINE

THINGS WERE A BIT EASIER with Allegra after
the rescue of Prissy's egg, especially since I managed
to bring back that stupid goose. I only got nipped
four times doing it. The best thing was Dr. B. told
Moonpearl she needed to stay until her babies were
born, even though her hoof was all healed up. I didn't
mind mucking out the stall anymore, because I got
to take her out to the pasture for exercise. Moonpearl
was so smart, I didn't have to use a halter or a lead
or anything; she would just follow me along the
path. I'd never seen a prettier sight than a unicorn

grazing in the meadow. Sometimes I had to leave her in the little paddock while I did other stuff around the clinic, but I always made sure I was the one who groomed her.

The money was nice too. Once in a while, I could get Steve to take me to the grocery store and buy things that I liked for a change, although he always seemed to find my box of Oreos, no matter where I hid them. Once he used the whole pack making piecrust, but he let me have half the pie, so that wasn't so bad. I bought carrots and apples for Moonpearl, and catnip for Timothy.

It was early November when Jamal Witherspoon and his mom brought in his dog, Butterfinger. She was a great dog, a big old golden mutt with floppy ears and a tail that was never still. Jamal got her for his birthday when he was five. He taught her how to shake and fetch and all. Every school day, she was waiting at the end of his driveway when he got off the bus. Since Grandma moved, nobody was ever waiting for me to get home.

Jamal and his mom were in the waiting room when I went to sweep in there that day. Jamal's mom had to take off work to bring Butterfinger to see Dr. B. She was lying on the floor at Jamal's feet.

"Hey, Jamal," I said. The dog didn't thump her tail at me. "What's up with Butterfinger?"

"She's feeling real bad," he said. "She quit coming to meet me at the bus, and she doesn't want to play Frisbee anymore. Now she's got this lump on her jaw and yesterday, she didn't eat, not even when I sneaked her a chicken heart." I could see he was awful upset about her. His foot was tapping a mile a minute, like it does when he takes a hard test at school. His mom looked upset too, and kept bending over to pet Butterfinger, making little shushing noises. I could see the lump close to the edge of the dog's mouth.

"Don't worry," I told him. "Dr. B. can fix her right up."

Georgie came into the room and said to Jamal, "Come with me." I went back to sweeping, making sure I got all the yellow dog hair out from under the bench where Jamal had been sitting.

My last chore of the day was putting out fresh water for all the patients. I went to check the cages and there was Butterfinger. She had one of those cones around her neck and near as I could tell, the lump was gone from her jaw. She lifted her head to whimper at me, then slumped back down. "Hey, girl," I stuck my fingers through the wires to scratch her head, and her tail gave a feeble wave. When I finished putting out the water, I went to find Dr. B.

She was in her office, doing something at the computer.

"That yellow dog, she belongs to my friend Jamal. Why didn't she go home tonight?"

"She was very dehydrated, Eric, so we're keeping her to inject more fluids and more nutrition." Dr. B. looked tired — more tired than usual, that is. "She'll probably go home tomorrow."

"Good, she's OK then."

"Not this time, Eric," Dr. B. said, real soft. "She had an abscessed tooth, which we pulled and treated, but she also has cancer."

"But I told Jamal you would fix her; you'd make her all better."

"The cancer has already spread; that's why her breathing is so labored. Treatment is expensive. She would need chemotherapy and maybe more surgery. It would require a long recovery time and would be painful for her. She's a young dog and has a good chance, but it still might not work." I couldn't believe what I was hearing.

"Can't you fix her anyway? You just got another one of those goose eggs; you must be rich now." I knew cancer was expensive, but people got treated for it all the time.

Dr. B. just shook her head. "It's not that simple. Those eggs pay for a lot, but not always everything we need. I'll send her home with some medications to make her comfortable, but that's all I can do unless the family decides differently."

"I could pay," I offered. "You could use that money for Butterfinger instead of paying me."

"That's sweet, Eric, but it wouldn't be enough, even if Mrs. Witherspoon accepted your offer. It's not just a matter of money. She thinks it is wrong to make Butterfinger suffer through the chemo, losing her fur and feeling much worse than she does now. She doesn't want her pet to go through that and she wants to spare Jamal watching his dog in pain. And we can't treat an animal without the owner's permission."

"I bet Jamal would give you permission. He loves that dog more than anything."

"It has to be from an adult. I'm sorry. It's the hardest part of this job, the knowledge that you can't save them all."

"You can't just send her home to die!"

"I'm sorry, but that's all I can do now," said Dr. B. I knew that voice, the one that adults use when they aren't going to talk anymore, no matter how unfair something is. I stood there a bit longer, but she just went back to clicking around on her computer.

In the recovery room I hunkered down next to Butterfinger's crate. She licked my fingers when I reached in to pet her. I had promised Jamal that we would fix Butterfinger. There had to be something I could do.

Then I remembered Moonpearl. One touch of

her horn had cured Timothy. Those unicorn hairs made Grandma's hands better. I bet she could help Butterfinger.

I checked the front desk — Georgie wasn't there. Then I heard her talking to Dr. B. down the hall. No sign of Allegra either. The kitchen was empty. If I was quick, I could sneak Butterfinger out to the barn and back before anyone noticed.

I quietly opened Butterfinger's crate. She thumped her tail at me, but couldn't stand up. I pulled the blanket she was lying on toward the door and eased her out of the crate. She whimpered a bit.

"Shhh, it's all right, girl, it's all right." I stroked her sides to calm her and felt her ribs all bumpy beneath my hand. I took the cone off her neck, but she could hardly lift up her head. I squatted down, wrapped the blanket around her, and picked her up. Even all bony as she was, she was still heavy.

I made it through the kitchen and cradled her on

one shoulder while I opened the door. No one noticed it clicking shut. I crunched across the gravel
drive and into the barn. The door was creaky, but we
got through. Butterfinger started a low whine.

A voice came over my head. "This barn has a cat; it doesn't need one of those things messing up the place." Timothy leapt from his perch in the hayloft onto a cross brace and down to the top of the stall door.

"She's not staying." I stopped in front of the unicorn's stall. Moonpearl came over to the railing and huffed a greeting. The lovely rose and new earth smell washed over me and the dog stopped whimpering.

"This is Butterfinger," I said. "She's real sick and needs your help." I laid Butterfinger down and slid open the door. Moonpearl stepped out, all graceful and calm. She turned her head and studied the dog. Butterfinger thumped her tail, which was a good sign. Timothy crept along the railing and crouched next to me, taking in the whole situation.

"Timothy, tell me if Moonpearl agrees to help."

"Then you will take this creature out of my barn,

preferably somewhere far away?" His tail lashed back and forth, which was not a good sign.

"She'll go back home, far away from here." I turned to Moonpearl. "Please, she's my friend's dog, and he loves her more than anything. Can you make her better?"

"Very well." Timothy jumped down to the floor, keeping well away from the dog. Moonpearl studied Butterfinger, who thumped her tail some more, and whined a bit, but didn't stand up.

"Are you sure you are strong enough for this, my lady?" Timothy asked. Moonpearl twitched her ears back at him and then looked at me.

"She says she will do it, as a favor to you."

"Sweet!" This was great! Butterfinger would get better, Jamal would be happy, Dr. B. could keep her old goose egg money for other patients, and I could keep my paycheck, too. A win-win all around.

I scratched Moonpearl on her favorite place,

under her chin. She pulled back and nuzzled my hand. "Thanks, beauty," I said. She took a couple of steps closer to Butterfinger, then lowered her head. Her horn touched Butterfinger on her side, very gently, near her heart. Light seemed to flow down the horn like water, and a strange humming feeling filled the barn. She held her horn there for maybe ten seconds, before shuffling back a few steps, her head still low.

Butterfinger shivered all over, then scrambled to her feet.

She gave three short barks, and jumped up to lick my face. "Pew, dog breath." Then I laughed out loud. It worked! Butterfinger was all better.

Butterfinger trotted over to the unicorn, her tail twirling like a helicopter. They touched noses. Butterfinger backed up and made that same funny little bowing motion that Timothy had when the unicorn restored his visibility.

"The thing has better manners than I expected," said Timothy. "Now kindly remove it from my barn." He retreated to the top railing of the stall.

I hugged Moonpearl's neck. "I knew you could do it, thank you, thank you!" She backed into her stall and I slid the door shut. She folded her legs, first the front, then the back, and settled into the straw bedding with a sigh. I gave her a carrot from my stash in the feed room. Her head was drooping a bit as she munched the carrot.

Butterfinger was frisking around, good as new. I gave her a big hug. Butterfinger had been dying and now she was fine. Maybe Moonpearl could do the same thing for Grandma — she wasn't dying, just old and crippled up. It should be easier to fix her.

We slipped out of the barn and up to the kitchen door. I opened it slowly and checked around — nobody in sight, but I could hear voices down the hall. I picked Butterfinger up so she wouldn't give us away with her toenails clicking on the floor. She licked my face as I put her back in her crate. "Shhh, go to sleep now." She stuck her nose through the wire to try and give me one last lick, then curled up on the floor of the crate. I turned out the lights and went home.

CHAPTER TEN

THE NEXT DAY AT SCHOOL, Jamal looked kind of down. I knew Butterfinger was OK, but I didn't say anything. Maybe if I went straight to the clinic from the bus, I'd get to see him when they picked her up. It would be so cool, Butterfinger being her old self and Jamal all smiles. Of course, I'd have to let Dr. B. take the credit, but it would be worth it. I was getting pretty good at vet stuff and this secret-keeping thing, too.

I bopped through the kitchen door and into the holding room. A cat was sleeping in a cage on the lower level, a parakeet sat on a high shelf, and the squonk water was swirling in its jar. I still hadn't seen it or heard it sing, but the water moved sometimes. Butterfinger wasn't in her crate. I guessed Jamal's mom must've picked her up already. Too bad, I missed seeing Jamal's face when he found out Butterfinger was all better. I got out the broom and dustpan and began sweeping. The sooner I got done here, the sooner I could go be with Moonpearl.

Dr. B. was standing in the doorway to the kitchen. She didn't look happy. She waggled her finger in that way that meant "come here." I stuck the broom and pan back in the closet and followed her down the hall to her office.

She sat down behind her desk and motioned for me to sit too. Timothy was perched on the edge of her desk, staring at me. I was beginning to get a bad feeling about things.

"So, Eric, Butterfinger looked much better this morning," said Dr. B. "So much better that I ran some tests on her and discovered that her cancer tumors were gone. You wouldn't happen to know anything about that, would you?"

Uh-oh.

Timothy suddenly began washing his paw, avoiding me. I looked down at my feet, trying to think of what to say.

"Have you been to the barn today?" the doctor said.

"No, ma'am."

"Then you haven't seen the unicorn."

I looked up. "No, ma'am." The doctor was staring at me hard, and Timothy was too. What was going on?

"She is weak today, and isn't eating." A spurt of fear shot through me. "You used her to heal Butterfinger, didn't you?"

I nodded. "Is Moonpearl going to be OK?"

"I think so," Dr. B. said gently. I relaxed back into the chair. Timothy was still staring at me. The doctor rubbed her temples, then looked back up at me. "Eric, what you did was wrong."

Wrong? How could it be wrong to make my friend's dog better? Moonpearl had magic that could make her better, make all the sick animals here better.

"We don't own these creatures, none of them, but especially the magical ones. If they are pets, they belong to other people and we can't do certain things without their owner's permission. Do you understand?"

"But Moonpearl doesn't have an owner," I said. "She can help all the other animals that come here. You could be the best vet ever, with her helping you, helping us."

"The unicorn is a wild creature; she doesn't belong to us. She has her own purpose. Even though healing power is part of that purpose, it seems that healing weakens her now. I don't know if that's because she is pregnant, or if that's how it always works. I just don't know enough about unicorns. We can't risk it."

"I didn't mean to hurt her! I would never do that!" I cried.

Timothy glared at me. "I told you that magic sometimes has a cost, a cost to the magic user. The lady is paying that cost now."

My throat got tight and my nose stung. Clenching my teeth, I looked back down at my shoes so Dr. B. couldn't see how red my face was.

"I know you didn't mean to hurt her," she said. "But we have a responsibility to these animals, all of them, to heal them, to keep them safe. Even if it doesn't harm the unicorn to heal, I can't use her to cure animals that other vets can't. It would be suspicious and draw too much attention, especially when the cures stop after she leaves."

Timothy jumped down from the desk and came over to rub his head against my leg. I reached down to stroke his back. I didn't see why Moonpearl had to leave. She liked it here. Timothy jumped into my lap, and I hugged him.

"Moonpearl doesn't have to leave. She can stay here and I'll take good care of her. She could use her magic only when she wants to. I asked her to heal Butterfinger; I didn't force her."

"It's true, the boy did ask. She did it as a favor to

him," said Timothy. I hugged him tighter, feeling the rumble of his purr. Timothy understood; he was on my side.

"Eric, once her foals are born and she's recovered, we have to let her go. She doesn't belong in a barn. Even if the unicorn stayed here, we would still be risking discovery. She's not like Timothy or Prissy. She doesn't look ordinary. No one must ever see her."

"No one will, I'll make sure of that," I said.

"We have to let her go," Dr. B. said. "It's not up for discussion. Now promise me that you won't use her to heal any more animals. You've kept the magical animals secret, so I know I can trust your promise. Do I have your word on this?"

"Yes, ma'am," I said.

"Good boy," said Timothy. "Now, scratch my left ear." I did, and the right one for good measure. Everybody in this place was so bossy. Except for Moonpearl.

"Moonpearl hasn't been groomed yet today," said

Dr. B. "Why don't you go do that?" She smiled briefly, then turned on her computer.

"OK," I said, letting Timothy go as I stood up. He hopped back up on the desk, then into Dr. B.'s lap.

I stopped in the kitchen to get an apple from the stash I kept for Moonpearl and cut it into slices. I could hear Georgie talking to someone in one of the exam rooms, but no sign of Allegra. She probably knew all about Butterfinger and my getting in trouble, so I really didn't want to see her at that particular moment.

As I closed the barn door, Moonpearl nickered to me. Her head was poking out of the stall, watching me. She looked OK and I sighed in relief.

"Hey, beauty," I said softly. I opened the stall door and slipped inside.

"Honk." Prissy flapped at me, and checked me out with one mean little black eye. The goose and the unicorn had become pals and the doctor let Prissy sleep in the stall sometimes. I gave Prissy an apple slice and she settled into the straw next to Moonpearl. I held out my hand flat with another apple slice on it. Moonpearl picked it up delicately with her lips, no teeth at all.

I fetched the curry brush from the shelf and began working down from her jaw, along the side of her neck and withers. She nibbled my sleeve, asking for more apple, as I brushed her rump. "All gone," I said, showing her my empty hands. Moonpearl snorted at me and turned to slurp down some water.

She did seem tired; the skin around her eyes looked darker, but I could tell she still liked me. Everything was going to be OK.

CHAPTER ELEVEN

THE NEXT DAY, ALLEGRA WAS in the barn when I got there. She was already combing out the unicorn's mane, even though grooming was my job. Moonpearl snorted, and I saw how glad she was to see me. It didn't matter if Allegra was there too.

Allegra looked over her shoulder, then moved over a bit to make room for me. I picked up the curry comb from the bucket and started brushing down Moonpearl. Her hair was thicker, now that her winter coat was coming in. That calm feeling settled into me as I worked.

"I heard about Butterfinger, you know, about how you got Moonpearl to heal her," Allegra said.

"So?" I said with a shrug. I kept working. Moonpearl's sides were bulging out more every day. It was getting harder to reach to the middle of her belly with the brush.

"So, I thought about doing that, too. Having the unicorn treat the patients. My mom works too hard. Even after the clinic is closed for the night, she stays up late, writing reports. She won't hire more help, because we never know when a special patient will show up. We've never gone on vacation, not even to visit my grandparents."

I didn't say anything. We didn't go off on vacations either; we couldn't afford to, although last summer Steve went to the beach for a week with his girlfriend's family. But I could see that the doctor couldn't leave if there were patients in the ward. She might be able to get somebody to look after Timothy; he was smart enough not to give anything away. But it could be bad if Prissy laid an egg around the wrong person, and forget about anyone else taking care of a unicorn or a squonk.

"Maybe Georgie and I could take care of things for a couple of days," I offered.

"Maybe. But it's not just that. It cost a lot to buy this place, and my mom still has loans from vet school. She's always worried about money, especially since my dad disappeared. I don't think we could afford to pay you."

That surprised me. "You got all those golden eggs."

"Only the shells are gold, not the yolk and the whites. I don't think she gets that much for one. She has to be careful about selling gold that pure. She mostly sells it to jewelers. Besides, Prissy doesn't lay eggs that often. I know that Moonpearl shouldn't be forced into helping, especially since it makes her so tired. Maybe it's just part of being a doctor—you're always tired." I hadn't thought of Moonpearl as a doctor, but I guess that's what she was, a sort of magical doctor.

Allegra pulled a bunch of hair out of the comb and let it drift down into the sawdust. I remembered the unicorn hairs Grandma picked off my shirt.

"I got an idea," I said. I told her about how the hair helped Grandma's hand. "I think there's power in the hair too, not just the horn. We could take the hair that we clean out of the curry brushes and combs and use that to help the patients."

Allegra looked at the comb in her hand. "You're right." That was a first, Allegra admitting I was right about something. "I always feel better just being around Lady Shimmershine Moonpearl." I could hardly believe she still used that stupid name. Allegra pulled another bunch of mane hair out of the comb. "Gimme your brush," she said, holding out her hand.

Same old bossy Allegra, I thought. She worked the comb through the brush, collecting a big fluff of unicorn hair. "That should do to start," she said. She tossed the curry combs into the bucket and ran out of the barn. I could hear her calling for her mom and Georgie as the screen door slammed.

"I better go see what she's up to," I explained to Moonpearl. It was my idea and I wanted credit for it. I patted the unicorn's flank goodbye and followed Allegra.

When I got inside, Allegra was in the ward room, eyeing the cages. "Mom's in the surgery and Georgie is assisting," she said. "Sewing up a tomcat's ear." She put the fluff of hair down on a counter next to a birdcage, then covered it with a paper towel.

"We could try it out," I said. "The ferret isn't doing so good; he could use some help." The ferret had been mauled by a couple of dogs when it escaped from the owner's house. With half its hair shaved off, a cast on one back leg, and bandages around its middle, it was a sorry-looking thing. Its breathing didn't sound good either, a raspy wheeze.

"What should we do, just put it in the cage?" she asked.

"I think the hair needs to touch him," I said. I took the towel off the front of the cage. The ferret was asleep, curled up on a pile of wood shavings, his tail curved over his leg cast. Gently, I pulled the cage off the shelf and put it on the counter where we could see better. The ferret jerked his head up a little, sniffed a bit, then dropped it back down. The card on the cage said his name was Slinkydink.

Allegra uncovered the hair, then rolled it down into a skinny lump. She opened the cage door and slowly reached in, then dropped the lump onto the ferret's side, between the bandage and the cast. He twitched and the lump slid off onto the bedding.

"That won't do anything; we've got to get it back on," I said.

"I know that," Allegra snapped. The lump was behind the ferret, on the opposite side of the cage door. "I don't want to move him and I don't want to get bitten." She pulled a pair of latex gloves out of a drawer and put them on. She reached in over the ferret, then stopped.

"I can't see it from this angle," she said. I could see though; her hand was close.

"Reach straight down," I said. Her fingers closed, but got only shavings. The ferret stirred and began breathing hard. She pulled her hand back out.

"The ferret is getting too stressed. It's not good for him," she said.

I turned the cage and leaned over and tried to blow the lump onto the ferret. That only blew a bunch of shavings onto him and made me sneeze.

"That was dumb." That girl never cut me a break.

"Got a better idea?" I said, brushing shavings off my shirt. More to sweep up later. Then the jar of tongue depressors caught my eye. I took out one of the flat wooden sticks and used it to push the lump of unicorn hair up against the ferret's back.

"What are you doing?" Dr. B. asked.

I jumped and jabbed the ferret with the stick. The poor thing flinched and raised up his head, hissing and showing me his teeth. I backed away from the cage.

Dr. B. stalked into the room just then and snatched the stick out of my hand.

"Mom, it's OK," said Allegra, jumping between us. "We aren't hurting him, we're trying to help."

"Get out. Both of you. Wait for me in the kitchen." I'd never seen her so mad.

We went into the kitchen and sat on the stools at the counter. I began to worry. Maybe I was going to get fired. I didn't care so much about the money, but what would I do if I couldn't see Moonpearl anymore?

Dr. B. came in after us and faced us over the counter. "Now tell me what you were thinking."

Before I could open my mouth, Allegra jumped in, explaining about my grandma's hands and the unicorn hair. I didn't even get to tell my own part of the story, but she did say the bit about the hair was my idea.

"Using her hair won't make Moonpearl tired, but it could make the patients better," I said. "We were trying it out on the ferret 'cause he's in such bad shape."

"You should have come to me with this idea first. The patients are my responsibility and I can't allow them to be experimented on," she said.

What did she mean now? In school, experiments are good things; it's what you're supposed to do to find out stuff. Moonpearl didn't need that hair anymore. What was the problem? Allegra looked puzzled too.

"But Mom, if it doesn't work, then it doesn't hurt anybody," she said.

"We don't know that. Also, you both know you aren't supposed to handle the patients without permission. There's so much I still don't know about these magical animals, what might be safe for them, what they might pass onto others. What if Moonpearl has some sort of virus that could infect Slinkydink?"

"But Timothy goes everywhere," I said.

"He doesn't go into the clinic rooms. He also lived with a family with other pets for a while before he came to us," Dr. B. said.

I hadn't thought about where Timothy was before.

"How do you know that?" I asked.

"Georgie brought Timothy to us. She found him as a stray and he lived with her and her pets for two years before he had his little visibility problem." The doctor laughed. "Georgie said she wasn't sure which was more shocking, that his middle was missing or that he talked. That's how she came to work with me and why we trust her with the special patients."

I was going to have to hear more about that story. I didn't talk to Georgie much, but I could probably get Timothy to tell me, with the right treats.

"Still, the idea of using the unicorn hair has merit," the doctor said. "Being around her definitely has a calming effect; I've felt it myself. And Prissy is much nicer since she's been sharing Moonpearl's stall."

"Great!" said Allegra. "I'll go get more hair." She hopped off the stool.

"Stop right there," said her mom. "Shaving off her mane or pulling out hair for our use isn't right. We will just use hair from grooming, nothing else." Doctors had more rules than teachers did. Still, I wouldn't want anyone pulling out my hair all the time, so I guess this one made sense.

"I'm going to go get the hair out of the ferret cage," said Dr. B. "You stay here."

She came back with the lump of hair held in the tips of a metal thing that looked like a cross between tweezers and scissors.

"The ferret is breathing much better, so perhaps this can work," she said. She was wearing a pair of rubber gloves. She took out a towel and laid the lump down on top of it. Then she opened a pad of gauze, put some surgical tape on two edges, turned it over, and put the lump of hair in the middle of the gauze. Using her fingers, she spread out the hair into a flat piece, instead of a lump. Then she rolled up her shirtsleeve and put the piece of gauze over a big red scratch that was scabbed over on her arm, smoothing down the tape.

Allegra burst out, "What are you doing?"

Dr. B. pulled down her sleeve. "I want to see if it helps this scratch that I got from the broken top of a cage. I also have a headache, a real one, not just because of you two." She gave us a hard stare. "If this heals the scratch in less than a day, then I will try it on the ferret." She straightened up, and collected the towel and the tweezer thingy. "Allegra, the tables in the exam rooms need to be bleached. Eric, you disinfect the empty cages in the ward before mucking out the stalls."

"Yes, ma'am," I said.

CHAPTER TWELVE

THAT LUMP OF UNICORN HAIR cured the doctor's scratch right quick. It was completely gone by the next day. I began collecting hair whenever I groomed Moonpearl, and Dr. B. let me make up little pads of gauze and hair to use. They were stored in a locked cabinet with some of the medicine. We didn't use them on all the patients, just the sickest ones, the ones Dr. B. thought needed the most help. The hair didn't cure everything instantly, like the horn did, but the patients got better a lot faster.

Moonpearl kept getting bigger around the

middle. Her skinny little legs hardly seemed strong enough to hold her up — she looked like a marshmallow on a bunch of toothpicks. Of course, I didn't say that to her. She was still the most beautiful thing I'd ever seen. I came over every day, even though I only got paid for a few hours a week. Dad was working late a lot and Steve was either working at the diner or hanging around with Darren and Charlie Deaton and that gang.

The Sunday before Thanksgiving, Dr. B. was in the stall, checking over Moonpearl, when I got there in the morning. The clinic was closed Sundays, so she had more time than usual, I guess.

"Morning, Eric."

"Morning." I snagged the bucket of grooming brushes and went into the stall. I stepped over the goose, who was snuggled down in the sawdust, and began combing out Moonpearl's mane. "When do you think the babies will come?"

"It's still hard to judge, but my best guess is mid

to late December," the doctor said, running the curry brush down the unicorn's withers. "It could be later, but I'd be surprised if it's later than New Year's Day. The foals are still moving a lot. Do you feel them when you're grooming?"

"I'm not sure," I said. Sometimes I thought I felt movement underneath the brush as I smoothed it down her sides, but it was hard to tell because the skin felt so tight across her belly.

"One of them is kicking now," said Dr. B. "Come here." I came around Moonpearl's front, ducking to avoid the horn. The doctor took my hand and put it on the underside of Moonpearl's belly, below the ribs. At first all I felt was the warmth of her soft hide and then, a poke, like someone knocking away my hand. Moonpearl turned her head to look at me, flicking one ear back at us.

"I felt it," I said. "I felt one of the babies move!" Dr. B. smiled at me, and I smiled back. There was another poke and I saw a bump move, pushing out Moonpearl's side just a little, like a foot moving under a blanket. I laughed out loud. The doctor laughed too.

"Mom!" Allegra called, appearing at the barn door. "Phone, emergency call!"

Dr. B. sighed and gave Moonpearl one last pat. "No rest for the wicked, even on Sundays."

Moonpearl tossed her head and shook out her mane. "Hey, I just smoothed that out," I said. I brushed her mane back so it all lay on one side of her neck. Her mane looked soft, but the hair was actually kind of thick and coarse. I finished grooming her and gathered up the combs and brushes. She huffed at me as I carried them to the bench, then nickered louder.

I laid out the brushes and took a regular comb, the kind people use, to tease all the hair out, collecting it into a big ball. I got out a bunch of gauze pads and put some hair on each one and stacked them up to use later.

Moonpearl nickered again and tapped the side of the stall door with her hoof. I turned to see what was bothering her. She craned her neck, trying to look around me to the bench.

"Oh, do you want to know what I'm doing?" I asked. She nodded.

"We found out that your hair has healing powers too. Not as strong as your horn, of course, and it seems to wear off after a while, like medicine you have to keep taking. It can help the patients and doesn't make you tired," I explained. I held out one of the pads with the wad of hair on it for her to see. She seemed to consider that for a bit.

"Is that OK?" I asked. Moonpearl made low rumbles in her throat and nodded again. The matter settled, she stepped back and nosed in her feed trough for a few stray bits of hay.

We were going to visit Grandma soon, and I was

thinking about how just a few little unicorn hairs helped her move her crippled-up hands. The hairs were gone the next time I went to see her and her hands were all curled up and stiff again. She would always check my shirt for hairs, saying she was looking for evidence I was visiting my "other white-haired lady friend." There weren't any, because now I made sure I had time to change my clothes before we went — Dad insisted we dress in our "Sunday best" for her.

Maybe I could take some and stick them on my shirt for her to find. I pulled some hair off one of the pads and stuffed it into the pocket on my T-shirt.

"Are more pads ready?" Allegra said over my shoulder. I jumped. Shoot. That girl could still sneak up on me.

"Here." I shoved the stack of pads with hair into her hands. She took them and then looked at me real sharp. She reached out and pulled the unicorn hair from my pocket.

"What were you doing with this?" she asked. "This is enough for another pad; you know we need those."

"Nothing." I snatched it back and spread it on a pad.

"You were going to take it, weren't you?" Allegra said. "Why? You're not sick." I could tell she was working herself up real good about it. Why did she have to be so nosy?

"I'm telling Mom," she said. She whirled and stomped toward the door. I couldn't let her do that; Dr. B. might think I was going to do something bad with it. I rushed after her and grabbed her arm.

"Wait, it's not what you think," I said. She pulled her arm away, but stood still.

"So, what it is, then?" she said.

I looked at my feet. She made me feel like I had been caught stealing. I was the one who figured out the hair had healing in it, not Allegra or Dr. B. That should give me some rights to use a little bit of it if I wanted, if I needed it.

"I want it for Grandma, for her hands."

"Oh. You told me about that. I guess I forgot, I was so excited about helping our patients," Allegra said.

"I was thinking if I could get her more hairs, use a pad of it, it would cure her hands, or maybe even her heart." *Maybe she could even move back home,* I thought.

"You can't just slap on a pad with unicorn hair, people would think that was strange," Allegra pointed out. I hadn't thought that far ahead, I was just focused on getting Grandma to touch the unicorn hair again. The best thing would be to have Moonpearl use her horn, but that wasn't going to happen.

"I have an idea," Allegra said. She went back to the bench and dumped the pads on it. She took one of the brushes and tossed another to me. "You groom her tail tuft, and I'll work on her mane."

"I already brushed her mane." Allegra ignored that.

"Hey, Lady," Allegra crooned as she slipped into the stall. Moonpearl blew out her lips, like making a raspberry at her. It wasn't rude though, it was just her way of saying hello. She stretched out her nose to me to be petted as I came in. So, of course, I stroked her velvety muzzle before moving down to her hindquarters. That tail was the only thing I didn't think was absolutely beautiful about Moonpearl. It just seemed she should have a long flowing tail like a horse, not this lion's tail thing.

"We need long, coarse hairs. Get as many as you can," Allegra said, running the brush through the unicorn's mane. I combed out the tuft on the end of her tail, and collected a bunch of long hairs.

"Give them here," Allegra said, holding out her hand. I gave her the silvery hairs. She sat on the stool by the workbench and pulled long hairs out of the brushes, then smoothed them flat. After bundling them up, she pulled a bead out of her pocket and slipped the bundle through the hole. She tied a knot in one end, then braided the hairs together. She tied a knot in the other end, fiddled a bit more, and held it up. It was a little white circle, a bracelet of unicorn hair with a blue bead in the middle.

"There," she said. "You can give her this and I'll bet she'll wear it. And the nurses won't throw it out, because she'll tell them it's a present from you."

I took the unicorn-hair bracelet from her and slipped it over my own hand. Some of the hairs stuck out and were a little bit scratchy, but it looked like those string bracelets a lot of the girls at school wore.

"It's nice. How did you know how to do that?" I asked. I couldn't help but grin. I just knew this would work. Grandma would be sure to wear it a lot, and her hands would get better, and she would get better. It didn't pay to think too much beyond that, but I could hope. Maybe she could visit for Thanksgiving, and Christmas too. This would be the first Thanksgiving that we weren't eating at the farmhouse, the first Thanksgiving without Grandma there. I wasn't sure what we were going to do. I almost forgot Allegra was standing there, until she spoke.

"I made friendship bracelets all the time, where we used to live," she said.

I could just barely hear her say, "Back when I used to have friends." I almost wanted to say I was her friend, but I didn't.

"Thanks," I said instead. It kind of meant the same thing.

Back at my house, I wrapped the bracelet in a tissue and stuck it in a little box that I kept a dead June bug in. I dumped the June bug out first. Even though I knew Grandma would like the swirling colors on its green shell just like I did, I figured they wouldn't appreciate June bugs at the nursing home.

I changed into Sunday clothes and went out on the front porch to wait for Dad and Steve. The little box was tucked safe in my back pocket. Dad came out and sat down next to me. He bumped my shoulder with his, and I bumped back. He fished a cigarette out of his jacket pocket and lit it with Poppaw's Zippo lighter. I liked the click it made when he flipped it closed. Dad blew a stream of smoke up into the air. The mintiness of the menthol didn't cover up the warm toastiness of the tobacco. I know cigarettes are all kinds of bad for you, but I sure did like that smell.

"Steve!" Dad hollered. "Get your rear in gear and get on out here." He blew another stream and bumped my shoulder again. "That boy can take longer primping than your mother ever did." I perked up at that. Our mom died when I was two and I don't really remember her. Dad and Steve don't talk about her much, and I hadn't heard that detail about her before. Then Steve came clomping out, calling, "Shotgun!"

"No fair, I was ready first," I cried, swiping at his leg as he went by.

"You snooze, you lose. You gotta call it," said Steve as he strode around to the passenger side of the car. Dad grabbed me in a headlock and messed up my hair. I yelled, "Cut it out," but really, I was too happy to care.

At the nursing home, the usual crew was out front, checking out all the visitors. The nurses at the desk waved as we went by.

Grandma had her eyes closed when we first walked in. She looked even tinier than usual, with the covers pulled up and her skinny little arms straight out on top. Dad leaned over and kissed her and her eyes popped open. "There's my boys," she said, her raspy voice hardly above a whisper. We had missed last week, on account of her hall was locked down because of the flu. They closed it off to keep the flu from spreading to the other halls, but I don't know if it helped much. Grandma hadn't caught it, but she still didn't look so good.

Steve clicked on the game. Football this time, the Panthers versus the Steelers. Soon he and Dad were ignoring us, as usual.

"How's my blue-eyed boy?" Grandma whispered. I sat on the bed next to her, my back to Steve and Dad.

"I got something for you," I whispered and pulled the little box out of my pocket. I held it out to her.

"You open it for me," she said. I took the lid off and picked up the unicorn-hair bracelet. "Now, where did you find that?" Grandma flicked her eyes over at Dad, then back to me. She held out her left hand, and I was just able to slide the bracelet over the crumpled-up fingers.

"I didn't find it; it was made for you."

"Was it now?" She held up her arm. The white bracelet hung from her skinny wrist. I held my breath, waiting for her fingers to move, to be healed. Slowly, she reached her other hand up, and one bent finger brushed the white hair. "By your other white-haired lady friend?" Grandma asked. The bent finger hooked inside the circle, then gently pulled away, straightening as it went. The bracelet was working!

"Not exactly," I said. "It's hair from that white horse I told you I was taking care of. Allegra, she made it." Grandma looked at me sharp.

"Allegra?" Steve broke in. "Who's Allegra? Hey, Dad, did you hear, Eric's got a girlfriend!" Steve poked Dad in the side and pointed at me. "Ah-lleggg-rah. She makes bracelets," he said, in a singsongy voice.

"Hush now, Steve. I didn't notice you bringing me anything from that girl of yours or even on your own account," Grandma scolded him. I tried not to let my grin show. She always did like me best.

Dad's big hand reached past me and took Grandma's wrist, the one with the bracelet. "What did you say it was made from?" he asked. Bending over me, he pulled her arm up higher so he could examine the bracelet. Grandma gave him a hard look and he let go.

"Just white horse hair. From the horse the vet's paying me to help take care of," I said. "Allegra's the vet's daughter, remember?"

"Right, that bossy little girl," he said. He sat back and quit looming over us. Sometimes I forgot how big he was.

Both Dad and Grandma kept looking at me. I squirmed a bit, wondering what I had done wrong. I could see the bracelet was working. Grandma was rubbing it between the fingers of her left hand and the fingers were straight and soft-looking. She got a determined look on her face.

"Eric, hand me that doohickey," she said, motioning to the bed control box. I handed it to her, and she raised the head of the bed to a sitting position, then straightened her robe and fluffed up her hair.

"Boys, I'm not spending Thanksgiving in this sorry old place," she announced. "You're going to carry me home and we will do it up right. Not only that, but we are inviting the new neighbors, that doctor and her child, to share with us."

"Yay!" I yelled.

"Now, Mama, are you sure that's a good idea?" Dad asked.

"All right, touchdown!" said Steve, paying no mind to us.

Grandma laughed. "You boys, what are you gonna do without me?"

CHAPTER THIRTEEN

THE NEXT FEW DAYS were real busy. We had to get the house ready for Thanksgiving. I guess we weren't too bad for a bunch of guys. We generally kept the trash off the floor, and Dad insisted that the dishes get washed every night. But it wasn't Grandma-clean, that was for sure. I was much better at house-cleaning stuff now, on account of the work I did at the clinic—all that sweeping and mopping and dis-infecting. But we still had a lot of work to do.

Grandma was calling the house every night, tell-ing Steve what to buy at the store, reminding Dad when to come by to take her to the beauty parlor to get her hair fixed, asking me to make sure the mantel above the fireplace was dusted, the windows washed. Allegra told me she called them too, making sure Georgie was coming and asking about their favorite foods.

I still went to the clinic every day. I couldn't stay away from Moonpearl. It seemed like she couldn't get any rounder, but she did. Even though Dr. B. still thought the babies would come in December, I was worried they might come while Grandma was here at Thanksgiving, and I would miss their being born. Dr. B. hadn't said I could help, but I had promised Moonpearl I would be there. Breaking promises is bad, but it should be double bad to break a promise to a unicorn.

Early Thanksgiving morning, I went with Dad to get Grandma. Steve stayed at the house, fixing the turkey. He had grumbled a bit about missing Thanksgiving at his girlfriend's house, but got excited when Grandma shared her pecan pie and stuffing recipes. He was getting pretty good in the kitchen, though not as good as Grandma.

"She painted the farmhouse," Grandma said as we drove past. "And look at that shiny new red tin roof!" I'd forgotten Grandma hadn't seen the place since Dr. B. moved in and fixed it up. She kept staring at it as we drove up the driveway to our house.

I wrestled her wheelchair out of the trunk while Dad helped her out of the car. We got her settled into the chair, and Dad backed it up to the front porch steps. "Close your eyes, Grandma," I said, as I held the door open so Dad could wheel her in.

"Close my eyes? The house can't be that bad, not if you boys have done what I told you," she said, but she covered her eyes with her pretty little uncurled hands. I caught a glimpse of the unicorn-hair bracelet on her wrist as the wheelchair bumped over the threshold. Dad wheeled her into the dining room and Steve came in from the kitchen.

"OK, open them now," I said.

Grandma lowered her hands, opened her eyes, and gave a little gasp. The table was draped with the tablecloth she always used for holidays, the fancy lace one. It was set with her best china dishes, her best glassware, and candles, too, just like she had always done at Thanksgiving.

"Oh, you all are the best boys ever," she said. I could tell she was happy. I just hoped she wouldn't notice that my place had a jelly-jar glass — I broke one of the good glasses when we unpacked them.

"Happy Thanksgiving, Mama," Dad said, patting her on the shoulder.

"It was Dr. B.'s idea to use these," I told her, wanting to be fair about the credit. I'd forgotten we kept all this stuff after Grandma moved out, until Dr. B. asked what kind of Thanksgivings we had, plain or fancy, so they would know how to dress. They were both, I guess — the table was fancy, but we were pretty plain, in our good shirts, but no ties.

"Well, it was a wonderful idea, doesn't matter whose it was," she said as she rolled up to the table. She tweaked the cloth a bit and switched the silverware around so the little forks were on the outside, then fussed with the candlesticks in the middle.

"Stevie, how is that bird? It smells about done," she said, going to take charge in the kitchen. "Open that oven door and let me see." Dad and I retreated to the living room to escape all the talk about cooking. Fortunately, the Brancusis showed up about then, before Grandma could find more for us to do.

Their arrival sparked a flurry of taking coats and arranging covered dishes. Georgie was carrying a big cake with chocolate frosting, Dr. B. had a wooden bowl full of salad, and Allegra had a glass dish with cranberry sauce. I was a mite disappointed in that, as it was the fresh kind, not the good kind out of the can. I was minding my manners, so I didn't point that out. We already had the good kind on the table anyway.

"Welcome, welcome, come on in and sit," said Grandma, motioning for everyone to come into the dining room. She wheeled over to the head of the table, where she always sat. "Eric, come pull out my chair," she commanded. I picked up the chair to take it away, but she said, "No, leave it. I'm going to sit in a real chair like a proper hostess." Then she grabbed the arms of her wheelchair, lifted herself up, and shifted over to the dining room chair. Slowly, she lowered herself down, smoothed out her skirt, and, like a queen, nodded for all of us to sit.

It was the first time since going into the nursing home she had taken any steps by herself. The bracelet was working, not just on her hands, but on all of her, like I'd hoped. If I got Allegra to make her another one, maybe she'd be strong enough by Christmas to move in with us, not just to visit.

"Let us all hold hands while Jimmy says grace," said Grandma. She reached out for Allegra and Steve on either side of her. I put out my hands for Allegra and Georgie. I caught Allegra's eye and then motioned with my head, so she'd look at Grandma's wrist and see the unicorn-hair bracelet, which she did. She gave a little smile. Then Dad asked the blessing.

When I raised my eyes back up, I noticed that both Dad and Dr. B. were staring at the bracelet too. Dad was at the other end of the table, with Dr. B. on his right and Georgie on his left. I quickly looked down so they wouldn't notice me noticing them; suddenly, my silverware was very interesting. Everybody began passing dishes and filling their plates, so I figured they would all just forget about that bracelet.

"Kris, I saw you painted the farmhouse and put on a new roof. I haven't seen the old place look so good in a long time," said Grandma. "Have you fixed up the inside too?" Uh-oh. I glanced over at Dad. He didn't like to be reminded that we had to sell the farmhouse and barn because we needed the money.

We'd kept the part of the land with our house and a few more outbuildings and all the rest of Harper's Woods. He didn't look too happy.

"I'm afraid you might not be as pleased with the interior changes," said Dr. B. "We had to do a lot to make the downstairs into a working clinic. That room off the kitchen is now our operating room for surgeries, and your old bedroom is full of crates and cages for our patients." She went on about all the new stuff, Grandma hanging on to every word. Then I got distracted by Steve kicking me under the table, trying to get me in trouble by getting a rise out of me.

"And who posted all those No Trespassing signs?" Grandma asked.

"I did," said Allegra, smiling at Grandma and making a "so there" face at me.

"Everybody knows there's no hunting on Harper land, but somebody might try to take advantage, thinking the vet here doesn't know. Good work, girl," Grandma said, but she was looking hard at Steve. He didn't hunt, but he had friends who did, and who were always pestering us about using Harper's Woods. He got busy chasing peas around his plate.

Then Grandma clapped her hands and raised them up. "Steve, fetch the desserts."

Steve jumped up, happy to be let off the hook. "Yes sir, General Grandma, sir," he said and disappeared into the kitchen. He reappeared with Georgie's chocolate cake in one hand and pecan pie in the other. He set them on the table, sweet as you please. Next, he came back with a plate full of peanut brittle — Grandma's recipe, of course.

She beamed, then picked up the cake server. "Who wants cake?" she asked. Her sleeve fell back, and there was the white bracelet.

"I'd love a piece of cake — Georgie's chocolate is divine — and that pecan pie too," said Dr. B. As she accepted her plate of dessert, she continued, "I couldn't help but notice your bracelet, Mrs. Harper, very unusual."

"Please, call me Maggie. Eric gave it to me. Said your Allegra made it for me, out of horse hair," Grandma replied, giving her wrist a little shake.

"Did she now," said Dr. B., all mild and sweet-like, while looking daggers at us.

"Came from that white horse Eric says he's

helping you with. His other white-haired lady friend, I call her," she said, running her hand through her own white hair. "Maybe I'll get to meet her too, when I come to visit your clinic. Nothing prettier than a little white horse, except maybe a blue-eyed boy." Grandma gave me a teasing smile.

"Maybe so." Dr. B. gave me a look that said I had a lot of explaining to do, then turned that same look on Allegra. We both shrank down in our seats.

"I'm beginning to think of this bracelet as a good-luck charm," Grandma told her. "I've been feeling so much better since Eric gave it to me, I hardly ever take it off." She had an expression that reminded me of Timothy when he's feeling especially pleased with himself.

Allegra gave me a look that said, *Do you think your Grandma knows about the unicorn?*

And I gave her one that said, *I don't think so. How could she?*

Dr. B. gave me a look that said, *She better not know.*

And then Dad gave me a look that said, *You better behave, boy.* There were entirely too many looks going around the table and not nearly enough talking.

"Maggie, could you slice me another piece of that pecan pie?" Georgie asked, breaking up the round of looks with some actual words. The conversation turned back to the desserts, as Steve tried to convince Georgie to give up the recipe for her cake.

After a while, Dr. B. stopped glaring at me and so did Dad.

Finally, Thanksgiving dinner was over. Steve and Dad were in the living room, arguing over which football game to watch. The Brancusis and Georgie were fixing to go, saying all their thank-yous and such. So I was hopeful that whole "white-haired lady" business was about to blow over. No such luck.

"Maggie, would you like to come over and see the clinic?" Dr. Brancusi asked.

Grandma got a big smile on her face. "Kris, aren't you a dear. I would love to come and maybe your girl can make me another one of these bracelets. A matched set would do me a world of good." She held up her arm and shook it a bit and looked straight at me. It was like she knew the bracelet was what was making her feel better.

Allegra was glaring at me, like I had spilled the beans. I knew I hadn't, so I glared back.

"Jimmy, I'm going over to the farmhouse. Come help me back into that fool wheelchair. You all go on, we'll catch up," Grandma announced.

I held the door for the Brancusis and Georgie, since their hands were full of dishes and containers of leftovers.

"No more bracelets unless you check with me first," Dr. B. said to me in a low voice as she stepped outside.

"Mama, you're going to tire yourself out. Are you sure about this now?" Dad said. But he could tell she was set on going, so he got her into her chair and then into the car. Steve decided to come too.

I sat in the back with Grandma and she took my hand as we turned out of the drive. It was the hand with the bracelet, and I noticed the fingers were curling up a bit again. Maybe the power of the unicorn hair was wearing off. I wished I could roll Grandma out to the barn and Moonpearl could use her horn to cure everything, so she would be strong again. That would be breaking my promise to keep everything secret and to keep Moonpearl safe, so I wouldn't. But I didn't want Grandma to go back to that old nursing home.

"Doesn't the place look grand?" Grandma said as we pulled up in front of the house. Dr. Brancusi explained about adding the ramp up to the front porch for deliveries. In this case, it made it easy for me to wheel Grandma up the ramp, while Dr. B. held open the front door. Timothy came and jumped up into her lap.

"Hello, you handsome fella," Grandma said, stroking Timothy's back. He purred loud enough for me to hear as I pushed the chair through the front door. Dad and Steve came clumping in behind us.

"Oh my," Grandma said, looking around the room at the bare floor and the desk and wooden benches. I had gotten used to it, but now remembered how proud she was of the living room, with all her best furniture, lace curtains, and framed pictures of Harper ancestors on the wall. This room was useful, but it wasn't pretty.

"Where's the clock?" asked Steve, and I realized he hadn't seen the place since Grandma moved out either.

"We have your grandfather clock and the sofa upstairs now," answered Dr. B. "We have a living room and a kitchen up there; the downstairs is all for the clinic." They bought some of the furniture along with the farm, as we didn't have room for much in our little house. Dr. B. pushed Grandma's chair into the office, explaining what everything was. I hoped it was clean enough. I hadn't done any mopping today—just fed everybody and groomed Moonpearl so I could get back and get ready for the dinner.

"So let's see what you've done with my old bedroom," Grandma said.

"It's our recovery and overnight ward," said Dr. B. proudly. She stopped the wheelchair at the open door. "We won't go in, I don't want to disturb them." Most of the cages were draped with cloth for the night already, but you could see the ferret cage and the jar of squonk water.

"I used to keep those kinds of things on the back porch," Grandma said. Then I remembered—she would keep barn cats with torn-up ears and baby birds that didn't have all their feathers out on the screened-in porch until they were better. She once had a baby squirrel, a scrawny little pink thing that she let me feed with a medicine dropper.

Steve stuck his head in and then came back to me. "Got a lot of weird stuff here, bro," he said. I was worried he might have figured out things, until I realized he just meant all the medical stuff. So I explained about some of the things I did, cleaning and fixing the food and all.

"So, you're a mop jockey," he joked, giving me a wimpy punch on the arm, but he looked sad. He had always been closer to Poppaw than Grandma, and didn't come here near as much as I did after Poppaw died four years ago. I guess he was remembering how it used to be, when it was all Harpers here.

"I've seen enough for now," Grandma said as she was wheeled back into the office. "I do confess, I miss my old living room, but you're doing fine work here, Kris. It all looks so grand." Her voice trembled and her eyes looked a bit watery. "I'm proud of you, Eric, for helping her. You're a true Harper."

"Come on, Mama, let's go," said Dad, real soft, as he took the handles of the wheelchair.

"Take me home, Jimmy," she said. She had never called Three Oaks "home" before—*this* was home. And now it wasn't.

CHAPTER FOURTEEN

DAD HAD ALREADY GONE TO WORK the next morning when I got up. Steve was still snoring, and he was planning to hang out with his girlfriend anyway. Nobody would notice if I spent all day at the clinic. I grabbed a bag of carrots and a couple of apples for Moonpearl and headed over. The grass was crunchy with frost and I could see the puffs of my breath as I ran.

The kitchen lights were on when I got there. Dr. B. was chopping up veggies to feed to the parakeet. There were empty bowls on the clean counter, waiting for the various types of chow — cat chow, dog chow, rabbit chow, ferret chow. I measured the food into the bowls, checking the daily feed chart to make sure I got the right amount. Nobody needed medicine with this meal, so it was pretty easy. I arranged the bowls on a tray and carried everything into the ward.

Attached to each cage was an index card with the animal's name, diagnosis, feeding and meds schedule, and owner's name. The tabby cat, Amber, hissed at me when I opened the cage and put in the food dish. I pulled out the water dish and put it on a separate tray for dirty dishes. Ajax, a bull terrier, was glad to see me and wanted to lick my hand, but couldn't figure out how to do that with a cone around his neck to prevent him from biting the stitches on his hind leg. His tail was thumping against the side of the crate, making a rattling noise.

"Hey, boy, glad to see you too," I told him, speaking softly so as not to bother the other patients. I scratched him on the neck and shoulder behind the collar and his tail thumped faster.

Dr. B. came in, carrying a tray with food for the birds. "You have a real gift for working with animals, Eric," she said.

That was nice to hear. I didn't get too many compliments. I took the bowl out of Ajax's cage and locked it. "I like them," I said.

"I can tell. And so can they." She moved over to the birdcages and lifted just the corner of the towel draped across one to open the door.

I fed the rabbit, then went to the cage that held Slinkydink. He was partially covered with the bedding. I opened the door and took out the old food dish, which was still full of ferret chow. That wasn't a good sign. The water dish was full too. I looked closer at the stretch of fur, but didn't see any movement. His back and ribs were still, no sign of breathing.

"Dr. B.," I whispered. "I think he's dead."

"Let me see," she said. She put on a pair of surgical

gloves, then reached into the cage and brushed away some bedding. The ferret's eyes were half closed and his mouth was slightly open. He still didn't move. Dr. B. pulled a flashlight out of her pocket and shone it on his face. The ferret didn't blink. She touched his side, checking for breathing, but still nothing.

"You're right. He's gone." She drew her hand out and sighed.

"But he was doing so much better," I said. "The unicorn hair was helping him. Look at his leg—you can't even see the scar where the dogs got him."

"He was doing better, but sometimes they decline very quickly. He must have died during the night, because I checked on everyone before going to bed," she said. She pulled off her gloves and threw them in the trash. "I'll have to call his owner. I hate it when they die during the holidays; it always seems to hurt even more. Not that a ferret cares about Thanksgiving." She gave me a weak little smile.

How could she smile, when this poor creature was

dead? She was supposed to save him. We were taking good care of him; he shouldn't be dead. It wasn't fair. I reached into the cage to touch Slinkydink. I ran my hand over his little gray body. His legs were all stiff, and his body wasn't warm anymore.

"He was hurt bad; we should have had Moonpearl heal him," I said.

"Eric, we've been over this. Moonpearl is an intelligent being, a wild creature, not a tool for us to use, especially now that she is pregnant. It took her several days to recover from healing your friend's dog. It would be even worse now that she's so close to delivery," Dr. B. said. She ran her hand over my head, like she was soothing one of the animals. "It's hard, but it's part of the job. We can't save them all." She left the ward and went into the office.

I finished collecting all the dirty dishes and took them into the kitchen. It had started out as such a perfect day, so peaceful, and now this. As I was scraping out the dishes, Allegra came in.

"The office door is closed. What happened?" she asked, leaning against the counter.

"Slindydink died."

"Aww, no," Allegra said. "Calling the owners to tell them their pet died is the worst. She hates that, always feels like it's her fault."

"Well, this one is her fault. Moonpearl could have healed him," I pointed out.

"Do you want Moonpearl to lose her babies?"

"No, of course not!" I said. How could she even think that?

"If Mom said it was too risky, then it's too risky, so we didn't do it," said Allegra. "Don't bring it up; you'll make her feel worse." Allegra stuck her head out into the hall, then turned back. "I'm going up to our kitchen to make her some tea. Why don't you go clean some cages or something?"

Nobody asked how I was feeling about finding a dead ferret. Sometimes this job really stunk.

CHAPTER FIFTEEN

THE NEXT COUPLE OF WEEKS were pretty good. Grandma was making plans for Christmas, telling us how to decorate the house and what church services she wanted to go to. Allegra made another unicorn-hair bracelet, so Grandma had one for each hand. We had figured out that the hair wasn't a complete cure, like the horn. It was more like medicine you needed to take all the time. Grandma must have worn the bracelets every day, because her hands got so much better that she started knitting again. I didn't even care that I had to go pick up yarn for her at Wal-Mart. Shoot; I used some of my own money to buy her this pretty greeny-brown mix that reminded me of Moonpearl's eyes. Figured it would make a good Christmas present. If she made me a scarf out of that, I might even wear it.

The Saturday before Christmas, as I was going over to the barn that afternoon, I noticed that the No Trespassing sign was gone from my treehouse oak. One little yellow-and-black corner was left flapping in the breeze. I checked along the property line, and sure enough, some of Allegra's other signs were gone too. I found one under a bush and another one next to the path. They must have come off during the storm the night before. It was still deer-hunting season, so I decided I would get more signs to post the next time we went into town, just to make sure.

A couple of cars were pulled up to the house, so I knew everyone would be busy with patients. I went into the barn to muck out the stalls.

Moonpearl gave a low nicker when I came in,

just to say hello. A new patient in one of the stalls, a nanny goat, started bleating, and Prissy started honking away too.

I tossed a bit of carrot to the goat, then opened Moonpearl's stall. She nudged my pockets, looking for her treats. She was so big now, she looked wider than she was tall, even counting the horn. I gave her a carrot and threw some little bits of biscuit to the goose.

"Is there a fish in that pocket for me?" a voice rumbled in my ear. Timothy popped into view, curled up on Moonpearl's wide back.

"No fish, but I didn't forget you," I said. I pulled out a napkin holding some pieces of ham and held it out to the cat.

"Don't think that makes up for interrupting my nap," Timothy said, but he gobbled down the ham anyway. He let me skritch his ear, so I knew I was forgiven.

Moonpearl swung her head around to watch me.

"Hey, beauty," I said, holding out another carrot. Moonpearl gobbled it up while I scratched her withers, the place between her shoulders. She liked me to do that. I stood there, scratching and breathing in that sweet unicorn smell, relaxing into the peace and quiet.

The stalls didn't smell so sweet though, and I got to work mucking them out and spreading fresh hay.

It was Saturday, which meant now I got to do one of my favorite things with Moonpearl — take her to the pasture on the other side of the ridge, just the two of us.

"Come on, Pearlie girl, let's go," I said, backing out of the stall. When Moonpearl came out, I closed the gate real quick, to keep Prissy inside. Moonpearl and me stepped out into the sunshine. The light rippled down her horn as she turned her head to watch me close the door.

She clopped around the barn and up the path. I walked behind her, watching that funny lion tail switching back and forth. The woods were a lot quieter in the winter than in the summer. There were no bugs humming. Not many birds singing either. Just unicorn hooves and my sneakers crunching through the leaves.

When we got to the pasture, I hugged her neck, breathing in that wonderful smell. She shook her head, breaking my hold so I would let her get to the sweet grass. I sat down and Moonpearl started to graze. Even though it was December, the sun was still warm on my back and arms. I could have watched her all day. If heaven was all the best things ever, this was heaven for me.

Moonpearl jerked her head up, laying her ears back. I had never seen her do that before. She snorted and pawed the ground, looking around the pasture. Trotting over to me, she whinnied and pointed with her nose back toward the path. She pawed my leg with her front hoof.

"What's wrong?" I asked.

Moonpearl scanned the clearing, shuffling her hooves. I couldn't see what had spooked her. She grabbed the sleeve of my jacket with her teeth, pulling on it.

"OK, OK, I'm coming," I said, getting to my feet.

Moonpearl pranced back a few steps, giving me room to stand. I opened the gate in the fence to let her out and we started back toward the barn. At the edge of the woods, Moonpearl stopped, her ears swiveling back and forth. I could tell she was listening hard. She started down the path, stopped, and looked back at me as if to say, "You need to come now."

As we entered the woods, it was much darker under the trees. I hadn't realized it was almost twilight. Every hundred feet or so, Moonpearl would pause, listening and taking in big breaths. Something in the woods was worrying her and that worried me.

We were almost to the top of the ridge when Moonpearl stopped and I stumbled into her rump.

Her head was angled back, but she wasn't looking at me. I spun around. Someone was behind us. About one hundred feet from us, a dark figure stood on the path.

Oh, no, someone has seen Moonpearl! Dr. B. will be so mad, was my first thought. I moved to try and block Moonpearl so he couldn't see her horn. He took a couple of steps toward us. "Hey, whoever you are, this is Harper's Woods. You're trespassing," I called out.

He gave a weird laugh that sounded like a cough.

Moonpearl shouldered me aside, lowering her horn. The stranger took another step toward us. Moonpearl snorted and pawed the ground. The stranger dropped down onto all fours. Big yellow eyes glowed in the dark. Whatever that thing was, it wasn't a person.

The thing crouched lower and stretched out a big paw, gently, silently, placing it down on the path. It moved like a cat, a really big cat. Closer and closer it crept, then snarled, flashing big fangs. It looked like a mountain lion, but mountain lions don't live around here.

Moonpearl screamed and reared up, her front hoofs striking out at the thing. It screamed back, clawing at her. I scrambled to get out of the way, but slipped on the leaves and fell. Moonpearl charged the big cat, her horn flashing.

"*No!*"

The cat-thing leapt off the path, fleeing into the

woods, and Moonpearl thundered after it. By the time I got to my feet, they were crashing through the trees.

"Moonpearl, come back!"

I ran, hoping to catch a glimpse of her. I could hear them for a few moments, but soon lost sight of them. There were no flashes of white between the trees and no sign of that awful cat-thing either.

"Moonpearl, come back, please come back!" I cried. I pushed through a tangle of bushes and vines, thrashing to pull my sleeve loose from a sticker bush. Everything was blurry; I had to rub my eyes to try and see.

My foot twisted and I fell flat, cracking my chin on a rock and biting my lip. I lay there, my cheek on the cold dirt. Maybe if I stayed still for a bit, Moonpearl would come back. But maybe the cat-thing would come back first. I rolled over and sat up. My hands were all scraped up, and blood trickled down my chin. I touched my lower lip — it was wet and puffy. My left ankle throbbed.

"Moonpearl!" I called again. No sounds from the woods. It was too dark to see very far under the trees. The pain from my busted lip made my eyes water. My ankle hurt, but I could walk on it. After wiping my eyes, I limped my way back to the barn.

CHAPTER SIXTEEN

IT WAS FULL DARK WHEN I got to the farmhouse. I dreaded telling Dr. B. what had happened to the unicorn, but she needed to know about the mountain lion or whatever it was.

Allegra was outside the barn and spotted me on the path. She came running, getting all up in my face.

"What happened to you?" she cried, taking in my ripped jeans and bloody lip. She reached for me, but I jerked back, avoiding her hand.

"Moonpearl's gone; she ran away!"

"What? What do you mean she ran away?" Allegra screeched. She shoved me on the shoulder. "She's about to have her babies! She needs our help. How could you let her do that? Why did you do that?" she yelled, and shoved me again. I let her. I deserved it. Moonpearl fought that mountain lion monster, and I didn't do anything to defend us. I was a coward.

"Answer me!" That girl was so mad, she kept jumping around, yelling, "Why?" I was afraid she would start kicking me next and I probably would have let her do that too. I tried to explain, but couldn't get a word in.

"Allegra! What are you doing?" Dr. B. grabbed Allegra's arm and pulled her back.

"He lost Moonpearl! I told you we should never have let him help! I knew we couldn't trust him!" she cried.

Dr. B. crouched down next to me and took hold of my chin, inspecting my busted lip. "Eric, is this true?" My throat was so tight, I could hardly speak, so I nodded.

"Tell me what happened," she said.

"We were coming back from the pasture, and someone was following us. At least, at first I thought it was a person, because it was walking on two legs. But then it snarled at us and dropped onto all fours. It looked like a big old mountain lion, but it couldn't be that, it had to be something magical. Moonpearl fought it and chased it into the woods."

"It sounds like a wampus cat," Timothy said. He twined around my ankles.

"What's a wampus cat?" Allegra asked.

"Legend has it that the first wampus cat was a Cherokee woman who changed into a mountain lion. Although why anyone would want to turn back into a human when you can be feline, I'm sure I don't know," Timothy explained. "Their usual range is in the mountains, so this is most troubling."

"Why is that?" Dr. B. asked.

"Such powerful creatures don't leave their homes without a reason. I have never heard of one in this area before. You were fortunate you were with the lady." Timothy's tail was lashing back and forth. He looked up into my face.

"They don't like men. Or boys. Few survive an encounter with a wampus cat. They are not kindly creatures. But they are also harbingers."

"What's that?" Allegra demanded.

"Harbingers announce the coming of an event or person. Wampus cats are death harbingers. Seeing a wampus cat means that someone will die soon," Timothy said.

"Does that mean Moonpearl is going to die? Or one of her babies?" Allegra cried.

And I had left Moonpearl alone in the forest with that. I pulled away from Dr. B. "I have to go find her, I have to find Moonpearl!" I couldn't let that wampus cat be right. I couldn't let Moonpearl die.

"I'll go with you!" Allegra cried.

"You're not going anywhere, either of you," Dr. B. said, grabbing each of us by an arm. "It's too dark to find anything in those woods now."

"But Mom, she needs us!" Allegra shouted, trying to pull away.

"Moonpearl has survived on her own all this time just fine. I doubt we could find her if she doesn't want to be found. If she wants our help, she will come back." Dr. B. pulled us in the direction of the house.

Allegra didn't look happy at this. I wasn't too happy about it myself. "But she needs us!" Allegra protested.

"Right now, what we need to do is have dinner. Eric, I'll call your father and tell him you will be eating with us. Now come inside, both of you," said Dr. B., her arms crossed.

"Yes, ma'am," I said. Allegra looked mulish, like she was going to say more, but she twirled around and fled into the house.

I picked up Timothy, rubbing my face on his fur

for comfort. I followed Dr. B. inside. She had me sit on a chair in the exam room so she could clean up my face. Timothy stayed on my lap, purring while she worked.

"It's not as bad as it looks. You don't need stitches after all," she said as she dabbed some Neosporin on my busted lip.

"Thanks," I said. Timothy must've decided I was all better now, so he hopped down. I washed my hands, inspecting the damage in the mirror. My bottom lip was still puffy and a bruise was starting to show on my chin. It looked like I had been in a fight, but I hadn't fought back at all.

Georgie was in the clinic kitchen, dishing out the evening meal for the patients that were staying overnight. As I helped her, I explained what happened, while Dr. B. went upstairs.

"I should've helped her fight that thing, that wampus cat," I told Georgie.

"It sounds like everything happened so fast, there wasn't anything you could have done. Besides, any naturalist will tell you that there is nothing more dangerous than a mother animal defending her own. Moonpearl was protecting you," she said.

That made me feel a bit better, that Moonpearl defended me because I was hers.

"Eric." Dr. B. was standing in the doorway. She looked serious.

"Did one of the patients die?" I asked. "Was it Tank?" Tank was a pit bull; he was pretty chewed up and Dr. B. suspected he was a fight dog.

"I talked to your dad. Your grandmother's had a heart attack and is in the hospital. He wants you to stay here tonight," she said.

"Is she gonna be OK?"

"It's too soon to tell. Your dad's going to stay there with her," Dr. B. said.

"She's gonna be all right though; she's coming

home for Christmas," I said. Could this day get any worse? First Moonpearl was lost in the woods, now Grandma was in the hospital.

"I hope so," Dr. B. replied. The clinic front door buzzed, and she glanced down the hall.

"Are you going to be OK?" she asked me.

I nodded, getting real busy with the dishes. She gave me a long look before leaving. Allegra and Georgie were both smart enough not to ask me about it. We all just went about our business, feeding the animals, cleaning up, like nothing was wrong.

We had dinner upstairs, in the new kitchen made out of my dad's old bedroom. It was strange, seeing his old closet turned into a pantry full of food and a refrigerator where his dresser used to be. Dr. B. made popcorn shrimp, my favorite, but I could hardly taste it.

Dad called after dinner. I wanted to talk to Grandma, but she was sleeping.

"She's stable for now," he told me.

"Then she'll get better soon — it can't be that bad, right?"

"I don't know, son. They're doing everything they can. Steve will come pick you up tomorrow evening and bring you over. You behave yourself, now." I said I would and we hung up. Steve was spending the night with his friend Richard; they were planning to drive to Charlotte for the football game in the afternoon.

Dr. B. made up a bed for me on the couch in the room they used for a den.

After I brushed my teeth and got under the blanket, Allegra came out of her room. She handed me a necklace with a big braided white disk strung on it.

"I made it with twice as much hair as the bracelets. Maybe if she wears it touching her chest, it will help her heart. You can give it to her when you visit."

"Thanks," I said, and slipped the necklace over my head. I held it to my nose and caught a faint whiff of damp earth and roses. Allegra must have gathered some of the hair that day for the smell to still be there. It made me feel a bit better. Surely Moonpearl would come back in the morning.

After Allegra went to bed and Dr. B. closed the door to her room, I lay back down on the couch, listening to the night noises of the house. It sounded different from when Grandma lived here. It had some of the same creaks and the grandfather clock was still ticking, but now there were some rustling sounds from the animals in the clinic.

I don't know how long I lay there, not sleeping, just fretting about Moonpearl and Grandma. Under the ticking of the clock, there came a soft humming sound. It got louder, the notes sliding up and down, almost like singing. It was coming from downstairs. I crept down the stairs as quietly as I could, but the third step from the bottom still creaked — that hadn't changed. The singing stopped for a moment, and so did I.

The humming started back up. Definitely coming from the clinic ward room. I eased the door open and peered inside. Tank was asleep in his crate. The birds had their covers over their cages. Across the room, near the window, I could just make out a dark shape in the glass jar of squonk water. There was a tiny swish, and the singing filled the room, sweet and rolling, like a lullaby.

I listened for a long time, standing there until my ankle started throbbing. I must have made a noise when I shifted my feet, because the singing cut off with a "bloop" of water. I waited, but the singing didn't resume. I slipped into the room.

"Hey, little squonk," I whispered. "I know you think you're ugly, but that was the most beautiful thing I ever heard."

I eased down on the floor, taking care not to jar my bad ankle, and rested my head against a cabinet. This had been the worst day of my life. But I got to hear a squonk sing. There was still magic here.

Tank was snoring softly. The room was warm. Dr. B. kept it hotter in here than the rest of the house so the animals wouldn't get chilled. It smelled like disinfectant, fur, and wet newspaper, the mix of things that came from taking care of creatures who needed help. I closed my eyes, breathing in those good smells.

CHAPTER SEVENTEEN

"ERIC, WAKE UP," SAID DR. B., shaking my shoulder gently. I opened my eyes, only to see the floor underneath the row of cages. It was pretty dusty under there, with little bits of kibble scattered around. I sat up.

"I must have fallen asleep. Dr. B., I heard the squonk singing! It was beautiful!"

"Really? I'm envious, I haven't heard it yet," she said, reaching down to help me up. I slipped in a wet spot on the floor and she caught me by the arm.

"Look." I pointed to a trail of water that led across

the room to the cabinet where the squonk jar was kept.

"We think the squonk climbs out of its jar at night sometimes. It must like you if it felt safe enough to come out with you in the room," said Dr. B. "Either that or you drool a lot in your sleep." She pointed to a big wet spot on my shirt front where the squonk must have touched me.

"Come on, you can help us with the morning feeding. Then I'll fix us some breakfast."

We fed the animals in the ward—mealworms and chopped fruit for the birds, kibble for the dogs. I sprinkled some fish food into the squonk jar, but it was still and quiet, not even a bubble rising to the surface.

"Did my dad call about Grandma?" I asked.

"No, not yet," said Dr. B. "That's probably a good sign. I'm sure he would have called if she got worse." That made me feel a bit better.

I took the dirty dishes into the kitchen and put all

the food away. I kept peeking out the windows, hoping that Moonpearl had come back. Allegra hadn't come downstairs yet. I guessed she did these chores most mornings, so I didn't begrudge her sleeping in.

"Let's go tend to the nanny goat and Prissy," said Dr. B. As she opened the screen door to the back porch, we heard a sound that made us both stop.

The sound echoed in the woods. Then it came again.

Gunshots.

And they were close. I didn't wait for Dr. B., just took off up the hill, ignoring the pain in my ankle. Moonpearl was lost and there were hunters in Harper's Woods. She was in danger because of me. I had to find her.

Everybody around here knew Grandma didn't allow hunting in Harper's Woods. But every few years, some hunters from Charlotte, morons who ignored the postings, showed up. At the top of the ridge, I stopped, listening.

"Eric!" Dr. B. yelled. She was coming up the path toward me. Timothy was with her. Another shot rang out, coming from the direction of the pasture. There was a road that cut through the property past the pasture and the cow pond. I bet the hunters had parked there and hiked into the woods.

"They're over there, toward town!" I yelled back. "We know where to look now. Let's go!" As I turned to follow the trail, Dr. B. grabbed my arm.

"Eric, I can't let you go into the woods when hunters are shooting out there. It's not safe," she said.

"It's not safe for Moonpearl either! If someone spots her, they'll think she's the white deer and they won't stop chasing her." I pulled my arm free and backed away from Dr. B.

"I'll call the sheriff. He will deal with the hunters. You have to stay here with us." She took a step toward me.

"No! You're not my mother, and you can't tell me

what to do!" I turned and dashed through the woods, slapping branches out of my way.

"Eric! Stop!" Dr. B. yelled. I could hear her chasing me, but I didn't look back. These were my woods, not hers — it didn't matter what part of them she owned; I knew them and she didn't. I cut over to the east and picked up the trail to the meadow. Dr. B. was still thrashing in the bushes.

At the creek, I slowed and walked alongside it until I came to the crossing rocks. It didn't matter if I left footprints; Dr. B. probably wouldn't notice them. I just didn't want to be splashing around in the water, because the noise might help her find me.

On the other side, I crossed the meadow to where there was a good thicket of bushes, low to the ground. It's where Grandma and me had found a fawn hidden one spring. I crawled inside the thicket to hide. I wasn't wearing camouflage, but my dark jacket and jeans were good enough. I drew my knees up, rested my head on them, and pulled my sleeves down over my hands. Now that I was still, my ankle started throbbing again, and I could feel the sting of new scratches on my face.

"Eric! Come back, please!" Dr. B. called for me. I didn't move. She came crashing up the hill, leaves crunching under her feet.

"Eerr-rick," she cried. I peeked out of the bushes. She was at the edge of the meadow. I could hear her breathing hard, like a dog after a run. She made a circle of the meadow and called again. I waited. After a few moments, she left, heading north, away from where the gunshots came from.

There was a rustle in the bush on my left, and Timothy stepped into my hiding spot. I put my fingers to my lips, hoping he wouldn't give me away. He sat up straight, curling his tail around his front paws, and blinked at me.

"As much as I respect the good doctor, I agree

with you. We must find the lady. We must protect her," he said softly.

"Thanks," I whispered. We sat there until I couldn't hear Dr. B. thrashing around anymore.

"Can you smell the gun smoke?" I asked.

Timothy glared at me. "I am not a bloodhound, but I don't need to be for this. The fools are this way," he said and slipped out of our hiding place. I crawled after him and followed the cat through the woods.

After a while, I realized we were close to Grandma's shortcut to town. Timothy trotted down a hillside to a road at the bottom. An old black Dodge pickup truck was pulled off to the side. We were on Harness Shop Road, not far from the county line. I checked the truck bed — there was a big cooler in the back and a couple of duffle bags on the floor.

Timothy crouched down near the front. "This way," he said and took off to the south, following

the road. I limped after him. After about a quarter mile, he left the road again. He was angling back toward the farmhouse, deeper into Harper's Woods. I caught up with him on a deer trail, waiting for me on a fallen log.

"Where to?" I asked.

"The smoke smell is strong here." He jumped down off the log and scratched at some leaves. "Look." He stretched out his paw and batted around one, then two bullet shells. "They still stink."

They looked like rifle shells, but I didn't rightly know. Harpers aren't hunters.

"Which way did they go?" I asked again.

"I repeat, I am not a bloodhound. Cats are stalkers, not trackers," he said peevishly. "Something big went blundering that way." He pointed his chin to the path.

I stepped over the log to follow it.

"Wait," Timothy said. "I hear something." He sat up tall, flicking his ears to the south. I could hear it too. I peered into the trees.

"Is it Dr. B.?"

"No, it's more than one creature walking," he said.

"The morons."

"I thought we were looking for hunters," said Timothy.

"Same thing." We followed the sounds. Finally, up the side of a hill off to my left, I caught sight of a patch of neon orange: a hunter's vest. I crept a bit closer, keeping a nice big tree trunk between us. I could see another flash of neon. There were two of them, hunkered down next to a big oak.

I was about to call out, when there was a rustling of bushes behind me. The rifles whipped around in my direction. I ducked behind the tree as two shots rang out. Peering around the trunk, I saw a flash of white near a thicket. There was another shot and a yowling sound.

Timothy! Those morons were shooting at Timothy!

I stepped out from behind the tree, yelling, "Hey, stop that!" when another shot burst out and something knocked my leg out from under me.

"*Aaaah!*" I screamed and fell back, banging my head on the tree trunk. "Stop! Stop shooting!" I screamed some more. My left leg was on fire. I grabbed my thigh and felt something wet—blood was soaking into my jeans.

"Oh, hell," a voice croaked. I looked up and saw

the hunters coming down toward me. It wasn't morons from Charlotte, it was morons from high school. Steve's high school, in fact. It was his buddies, Darren and Charlie Deaton.

"Oh, hell, Eric. What are you doing out here?" said Darren.

"Getting shot!" I screamed at him. "What are you doing here?"

"Sorry, man. Oh, Christ, I didn't mean to shoot you. Sorry, sorry, sorry," he said, stumbling toward me.

Charlie dropped down next to me and pulled my hand away from my leg. My jeans were ripped and there was a gash on the outer side of my thigh.

"It doesn't look deep," he said. He put his hand under my thigh and I gasped. "I think the bullet just grazed your leg." He pulled his scarf off his neck and began wrapping it around the wound.

"Oh, man, oh, man, so so sorry," Darren kept saying, waving his hands around.

"You know Harper's Woods are posted! You're trespassing!" I yelled at him. Yelling helped me keep from crying.

"Bobby Knapp saw the white deer last night, out on Harness Shop Road. He was telling everybody at the diner this morning. I didn't mean to shoot you, Eric, honest. We saw the white deer about an hour ago. Just now I saw something white moving down there. That's what I shot at," said Darren.

"That was Dr. Brancusi's cat, you idiot!" I said. "Look!" I pointed down the hill to Timothy, perched on a big rock, calmly licking his shoulder.

"Aw, no way, man, I swear we saw the deer," said Darren.

"Darren," said Charlie softly. "Shut up." He finished tucking the scarf around my leg. "We've got to get Eric to a doctor." Darren nodded, looking like he might throw up.

"Eric, can you stand?" Charlie asked. He held out his hand to me. I took it and pulled myself up. When

I put my left foot down, I hissed at the pain. When I tried to take a step, it buckled beneath me. "Whoa, steady," Charlie said as he caught me. I had been doing way too much falling down recently and I didn't care for it.

"Here, I'll carry you piggyback." Charlie crouched down in front of me. I put my arms around his neck and with a little hop, got one leg up. He tucked his hands under my knees and settled me on his back. It hurt to bend my left leg.

"Get the gear," Charlie told Darren. Darren scurried back up the hill and collected their guns. Charlie carried me down, and as we passed Timothy, the cat pointed with his chin. I looked back, past Darren stumbling down with the rifles and backpacks. There, at the top of the ridge, stood Moonpearl, white and shimmering.

Charlie stumbled a bit, his grip shifting. Pain flared up my leg. Then everything went black.

CHAPTER EIGHTEEN

I CAME TO WHEN WE GOT to the hospital. My leg was throbbing, but the scarf-bandage had stopped the worst of the bleeding. I was still so tired I could hardly open the door of the truck. Charlie came to the passenger side and gave me another piggyback ride into the emergency room and up to the desk. Darren came trailing behind.

"Mr. Harper." Charlie dropped my legs. I gasped as I landed on my bad ankle and jarred the gunshot wound. I sagged against his back.

"Dad?" He was standing there at the desk, looking like thunder.

"Your brother called me, said the Deaton boys were bringing you here," he growled, giving the brothers a hard stare.

"I called Steve after we got you in the truck," Charlie explained to me.

"Let's get you taken care of, Eric. I'll talk to you boys later," he said, glaring at them. He scooped me up and followed the nurse back to one of the beds with the curtain all around. Dad set me down on the bed. I lay back and started to pick at Charlie's scarf where it was tied around my leg.

"You want to tell me what you were doing so deep in the woods during hunting season?" Dad asked me.

"Ah, Allegra's cat got out and had run off into the woods. She and Dr. B. were worried, so I offered to go find him," I said. "Good thing I did, too. The Deaton boys were shooting at him—thought a little white cat was the white deer." It was close enough to the truth that it should work. The Deaton boys saw Timothy, so that part of the story would match up.

Lucky for me the doctor showed up right then, so I didn't have to hear what Dad thought about that just yet.

"Let's see what we have here," the doctor said, unwrapping the scarf.

The doctor cut off my jeans and cleaned the wound. It was only about three inches long, and not too deep for all that bleeding. The bullet just carved a chunk out of my leg, and kept going. The antiseptic stung some, but my leg didn't look so bad cleaned up. My ankle was puffy from where I twisted it.

"I'm going to find those boys," Dad said and left.

"Want to tell me how you got this?" the doctor asked, inspecting the gunshot wound.

"Hunting accident."

"Ah, well, 'tis the season," the doctor said. "You will need a tetanus shot then."

"I got one earlier this fall. I needed it so I could help out at the Brancusi Animal Clinic," I explained.

"So you are a fellow professional. We will check your records for that shot. Meanwhile, you are going to need some stitches," he said. He left for a bit and came back with a nurse and a tray of stuff.

He stitched me up, but his stitches weren't as small and neat as Dr. Brancusi's. I didn't tell him that though, on account of the pain medicine was making me drowsy. He packed and bandaged the wound, just like Dr. B. packed the cuts on that pit bull. Then he wrapped my ankle, which he said was just sprained, in an Ace bandage. I missed the tongue-lashing that Dad gave the Deaton boys, but I figured my turn was coming.

The nurse gave Dad instructions on how to change the dressing and clean the wound, even though I told them I could do it myself. He said the stitches would dissolve on their own in a few weeks. They loaded us down with a bunch of gauze and prescriptions and all. The nurse helped me into a wheelchair and gave me a little blanket to cover my legs while Dad finished with the paperwork.

It also gave me time to wonder how Dad got here ahead of us. I didn't much like the answer when I found out.

"Your grandmother had another heart attack early this morning," he said.

"Is she going to be OK? Can I see her?" I asked.

"I don't know. The doctor said there was a lot of damage to her heart," he said. That's when I noticed he was looking just as rough as I felt.

"She woke up while you were getting treated," Dad said. "She's been asking after you, so I'll take you to see her."

He wheeled me to her floor. I thought about trying to walk into her room, but then remembered I didn't have any pants on. Explaining about the accident would be less embarrassing than walking around in my underwear.

She was in a private room, hooked up to lots of monitors, IVs and such, with one of those little oxygen tubes clipped to her nose. Her eyes were closed and she looked pale. Her unicorn-hair bracelets were gone too.

"Mama, here's Eric to see you," Dad said as he wheeled me in.

"My favorite blue-eyed grandbaby," she whispered. "Where are my kisses?"

"Hey, Grandma," I said. I leaned over and gave her a kiss on the cheek. She opened her eyes and smiled. Dad leaned in from the other side of the bed and gave her a kiss, too. Then she went into a coughing fit. It curled her up like an inchworm and her face got red. Finally she stopped and waved at the water glass on her tray. I poured her a cup and helped her drink it.

Then my stomach growled.

"Jimmy, you need to feed this boy," she said. That's when I realized I hadn't eaten since yesterday.

"I missed breakfast this morning," I said.

"Seems you missed lunch, too. I'll fetch something from the cafeteria," Dad offered.

"Now, Eric, want to tell me what happened to your pants?" Grandma said.

So I told her my story about Timothy and the Deaton boys.

"I know your dad's right upset, but you did good," she said. "There always needs to be a Harper to protect Harper's Woods." She took my hand. Her fingers were cold. "And your white-haired lady friend, the pony, she's all right too?"

"Yeah, she's fine. She should be having her babies soon," I said. I hoped Moonpearl would come back. She hadn't run too far. Maybe when the word got out about Darren shooting me in the leg and the white cat in the woods, people would stay away. I hoped the gunshots had scared off the wampus cat and that Moonpearl would be safe, even if she didn't come back to the barn.

That reminded me of the pendant. I reached under my shirt—it was still there. I pulled it out and took off the necklace. Maybe that was why I could run fast enough to get away from Dr. B. in the woods —because the pendant had helped my bad ankle. I hoped it still had enough power to help Grandma, too.

"Allegra made this for you, since you liked the bracelets so much," I said.

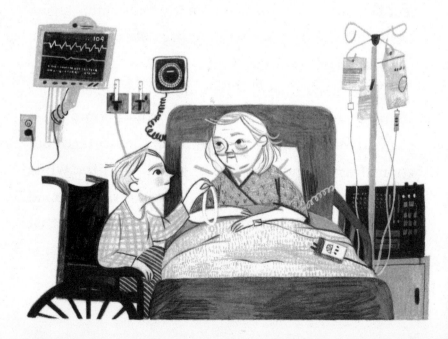

"Did she now? She's a sweet girl." I had never thought of Allegra as sweet, but she was nicer to Grandma than she was to me. I couldn't get the necklace over her head, what with all the tubes.

"I'll just hold on to it for now," said Grandma. "I'll put it on later. They don't like you to wear jewelry here in the hospital anyway."

"Dr. B. said I could watch the foals being born," I told her, to head off any questions about the hair pendant.

"That's good, that's real good. You love all God's creatures, just like me," Grandma said. "I knew you would be the one."

"The one what?" I asked.

"You'll find out soon enough," she replied, taking my hand. "Now tell me about what else you've been doing." So I told her about Tank and school and other stuff until Dad came back with some lunch. I ate a soggy tuna-fish sandwich and some limp

French fries while Dad watched a football game on the TV and Grandma dozed. It wasn't so bad. It was almost like a Sunday at the nursing home, but with more beeping machines.

CHAPTER NINETEEN

DAD GAVE ME A PIECE of his mind on the way home. About how stupid it was to go into the woods when I heard gunshots, that a cat can take care of itself, how I knew better and was in big trouble for not minding Dr. B., for scaring the pants off him (even though I was the one who ended up with no pants), how he had enough to worry about without my being a fool. It was a pretty big piece and I deserved every bit of it. With the painkillers working on me and hardly any sleep the night before, it was all I could do to stay awake to hear his lecture. When we finally got home, I went to bed and didn't get up until Monday afternoon.

When I did wake up, Allegra was sitting next to my bed. Wasn't sure I liked this development, especially once I realized that I still didn't have any pants on. At least I was under the covers. I pulled them up higher.

"I heard what happened," she said. "Timothy said you saw Moonpearl."

"Yeah, yeah, I did," I replied, sitting up a bit. "The Deaton boys didn't find her. She looked OK."

"Mom said I should apologize to you for pushing you and being so mean yesterday."

"OK."

"OK," she said. "Are you going to be able to come back and help at the clinic? We got three new boarders: a cat that lost all the skin and fur off his tail, a dog with a broken leg, and a chameleon with some weird eye disease."

I knew we were cool then, even though it wasn't much of an apology.

Steve popped in after she left to rag on me about having a girlfriend. He was stunk out that he missed all the excitement, although pleased at having something to lord over the Deaton brothers, especially Darren, who could be kind of a jerk.

Grandma was still in the hospital. Steve and Dad went to see her that evening, but she told them to make me rest. So I did.

Dad let me stay home from school the next day too, after making me swear not to go into the woods for the rest of the season. I promised, even though I was still worried about Moonpearl. I hoped the wampus cat was wrong, that Moonpearl wouldn't die and that it was far away from Harper's Woods by now.

My leg didn't hurt much at first, so I was able to get up and fix myself a peanut butter and banana sandwich. I had a cane to help with walking, but I didn't need it in the house. After lunch, I was tired of TV, so I decided to see if I could make the walk over to the clinic. I had to rest on the way by leaning against my treehouse tree, but it wasn't too bad. The cane really helped with the rougher parts of the path, though I didn't like to admit it.

Georgie let me in the kitchen door and swept me up in a great big hug.

"Oh, Eric, I'm so glad to hear you are all right. Timothy told us all about it," she said. I was beginning to think Timothy was a blabbermouth. She set me up at the counter with a stool to keep the weight off my leg and had me chopping vegetables and washing dishes. She went up to the front to help Dr. B. It felt good to be back, even if I was in for a come-to-Jesus talk from Dr. B., too.

I was just fixing to go check on the squonk when Timothy came in.

"You need to come outside," he said, then darted out the cat flap in the kitchen door.

I hopped down the back steps on my one good leg and looked around. I could hear a car coming up the drive, probably another patient. Timothy hissed at me, then disappeared around the corner of the barn. I followed. There was Timothy, sitting up straight and pretty, tail wrapped around his paws and his head tipped up. I'd left my cane behind in the kitchen, so I hobbled to the back of the barn and turned the corner to find out what he was looking at.

It was Moonpearl.

"You came back!" I cried. I hugged her neck. She nudged my arm and snorted a bit. She still had that same sweet smell, of roses and fresh-turned earth. That wonderful unicorn peace washed over me.

"I missed you so much," I whispered. She nudged me again, a shiver going along her skin. I stepped back to get a good look at her. Her mane was all scraggly and full of twigs, and her legs were muddy.

"Let's get you inside and cleaned up, OK?"

She nickered.

"She approves of that idea," said Timothy.

"Let's go in through the paddock. Less chance of being seen that way," I said. I took her through the gate, then scouted for civilians. Dr. B. had installed a fence across the driveway to stop pet owners from driving to the back of the house, but sometimes they parked in front of the gate. The coast was clear.

When I opened the barn door for Moonpearl, Prissy started making a racket, honking a welcome. Moonpearl bent her head down and snorted, resting her nose on Prissy's back. The goose honked once more, then settled down into her nest. Moonpearl was hidden from prying eyes and back where she belonged, with us.

"Timothy, go tell Dr. B. and Georgie that Moonpearl is back."

"Do I look like a messenger?" Timothy said with a sniff. He leapt up onto the edge of the stall door and looked down his nose at me.

"No, but I want to feed her and get her cleaned up," I said.

"Very well, that is something you can do better than I," he admitted and left.

I hobbled over to the storage room and scooped some feed into a bucket. My leg throbbed a bit as I carried it back into the stall and filled her trough. Prissy got underfoot, searching for spilled bits of grain. Moonpearl huffed, then nudged my arm. I felt bad that I didn't have an apple or a carrot for her, but I didn't want to leave her, not even long enough to find her a treat.

I fetched the curry combs and a soft cloth to wipe off the worst of the mud. Moonpearl heaved a big sigh as I ran the brush over her withers. The dirt was deep into her winter coat, but as I worked, she was getting back her shine.

There were three long scratches, already scabbed over, on the right side of her chest. I cleaned them with a wet cloth. They didn't look too bad, but I would have to tell Dr. B., so we could put some antibiotic ointment on them.

"Did the wampus cat do this?" I asked, tracing alongside the scratches. She gave a little snort and shifted her feet, so I figured I had guessed right about that.

"I'm so glad you're back," I said. "I'm sorry I left you. I should have helped you with the wampus cat and I should have looked until I found you that night. You could have gotten hurt by those knuckle-headed Deaton boys." I got the cloth and ran it down her front legs, one after the other. Moonpearl kept shifting her weight, lifting a foot up a bit and putting it down.

"What's the matter, sweetheart?" I had never seen her this restless before. She wasn't eating any of the feed either. Maybe she was thirsty. I left the stall to get her a bucket of water. She snorted a bit more and turned in a big circle, almost like a dog getting ready to lie down to sleep.

I got another comb and began untangling her mane, being careful not to pull too hard. "That's bet-ter, isn't it, pretty girl," I said in a soft voice. Avoiding her horn, I combed out her fetlock. Several long hairs came loose and stuck in the comb. I gathered them up and put them in my shirt pocket to save for later.

With the softer brush, I smoothed down her coat, starting with her neck. As I brushed her side, her skin gave a strange shiver. Afraid I had scratched her too hard, I stepped back.

"Did I hurt you?"

Her sides heaved again. Then it hit me. She was in labor.

"Are your babies coming?" I whispered. Moonpearl tossed her head and then turned and looked me in the eye. I took that as a yes, and hobbled as fast as I could to get Dr. B.

CHAPTER TWENTY

"WHERE'S DR. B.? MOONPEARL'S HAVING her babies!" I yelled as soon as I saw Georgie. She was loading a bunch of blankets and towels from the cages into the washer on the back porch.

"How wonderful!" she said. "Kris is in with a patient, but I'll tell her as soon as she is free."

"But Moonpearl needs her!" I said.

"Was she lying down yet? Could you see the foal?" Georgie asked.

"No."

"Then we have some time. Mothers usually want

some privacy. Why don't you go to the barn, but watch from outside the stall. It could be several hours before the foal presents itself. If Moonpearl seems in distress, come back for the doctor." Georgie waved me off the porch.

Moonpearl didn't look at me when I peered into the stall. She was standing quietly, with her head lowered. Prissy the goose was fluffed out in her nest in the corner.

After about twenty minutes with nothing much changing, I heard the front door to the barn slide open and Dr. B. stepped in.

"How is she?" Dr. B. whispered as she came and stood next to me, looking at the unicorn.

"Fine, I guess," I whispered in return.

Dr. B. stepped into the stall, moving real quiet and slow, motioning for me to stay put. She murmured something soft that I couldn't quite catch, and Moonpearl shuffled her feet a bit. Dr. B. ran her hands down the unicorn's side and moved to her rear. She lifted the unicorn's tail, then slowly lowered it again and gave Moonpearl another little pat on the rump. She came back to stand next to me.

"You were right, she is in labor, but it could still be some time before the foals are born. Can you stay for a while? I still have patients waiting that I need to tend to," she said.

"I'm not going anywhere."

Dr. B. got a lawn chair out of the storage area of the barn and set it up for me by the stall door. "Things will go better if she has some space and quiet. Come get me when she lies down or if she seems to be having trouble," she said.

I watched Moonpearl for a while, but nothing much happened. It was cold in the barn, so I got a blanket and draped it over her back. I found a smaller one for me and settled in the chair to watch. Timothy jumped onto my lap and curled into a fuzzy ball.

I must have dozed off, because it was dark outside when Allegra came into the barn.

"I brought you something to eat. Georgie made it before she left. She called your dad and told him you're spending the night here," she whispered, handing me a sandwich and a mug of hot chocolate. I had never heard that girl whisper before.

"Georgie isn't going to come watch the babies being born?" I asked. I couldn't understand how anyone could miss this.

"She said someone needed to get a good night's sleep," Allegra said. She peered into the stall, then sat down next to me. Timothy decided he liked her lap better.

"Thanks," I said. We sat there while I munched on my sandwich, Allegra still quiet for a change.

Moonpearl made a strange grunting noise. She stamped her feet, turning in circles. She chuffed at Prissy, turned some more, and moved to the far side of the stall. Then she knelt down, first her front legs, then her back, and slowly rolled over onto her side. There was a big wet spot on the hay next to her tail.

Allegra shot up, dumping Timothy off her lap. She ran into the stall, and I followed right behind her. Moonpearl didn't even raise her head to look at us. Just below her tail, I could see a white sac, with something dark inside.

"They're coming! I'll go get Mom!" she said, still whispering, and left.

Moonpearl gave another grunt and the sac slid out farther. I could see legs inside. It was finally happening; she was having her babies. Moonpearl was breathing heavily. "You're doing great, girl," I said softly. I kept whispering to her, telling her everything would be all right. Timothy had disappeared.

The barn door opened and Dr. B. and Allegra came in. Dr. B. had her box of medical stuff and Allegra had an armful of towels. Prissy hissed at them.

Dr. B. knelt down next to Moonpearl. She put on a pair of rubber gloves and checked the sac. She took a bottle out of the box, poured some stuff onto a towel, and wiped around under Moonpearl's tail. Prissy flapped her wings and began honking.

"She's doing fine. Allegra, can you take Prissy and put her in the next stall?" she asked. I was glad Allegra was the one stuck with that job. Allegra swooped up the goose and clamped her hand around her beak. Prissy wriggled, but Allegra didn't let go. They brushed past me. I retreated to the far side of the stall, out of the way.

Moonpearl made another grunt.

"Good girl, won't be long now," murmured Dr. B. I could see the shape of the foal's head inside the white sac now. Moonpearl gave another big shiver all down her body. The foal was wiggling around, then a foot poked out. Dr. B. moved back a bit. The foal slid all the way out.

"There you are, you little beauty," said Dr. B.

The baby wasn't white; it was dark, almost black. It blinked its eyes at me. After checking over Moonpearl, Dr. B. gently removed the rest of the birth sac from the foal.

"It's a girl," she said softly. "Eric, bring some of the towels and wipe her down. She should be trying to stand up in about ten minutes or so. I need to make sure the second delivery goes well too."

I crouched down next to Moonpearl, spreading out one of the towels. Dr. B. lifted up the foal and moved her onto the towel, so she would have more room to work. Using another towel, I began wiping the foal's neck. She was so warm! She felt lots warmer than Moonpearl usually did. Her coat was wet and bits of the sac were still clinging to her back legs.

She raised her head, then rolled over with her chest down and her legs sprawled out. I wiped her body, very gently. Her head was really wobbly as she turned to look at me, and I realized she didn't have a horn. Her eyes were big and dark, and she had really long eyelashes.

"Hey there, happy birthday," I said softly.

Allegra sat down next to me and started rubbing down the foal's back legs. "Isn't she beautiful?" she whispered.

"Yeah, but is she really a unicorn? She doesn't have a horn," I pointed out.

"Cows aren't born with horns, and deer aren't born with antlers. Makes sense that unicorns would be the same," said Dr. B. "Can you give us a bit more room?"

I scooted back as best I could, pulling the towel with the baby unicorn on it. Allegra shifted over with us. She took another towel and wiped down the foal's tail, which was the same as her mother's, sort of a lion tail with a tuft, but shorter.

"Eric, you need to give the baby room too. She needs to be able stand up on her own," said Dr. B.

I pushed back farther and bumped into the side of the stall, which sent a pain shooting through my bad leg. I bit my lip to keep from making any noise that would upset Moonpearl.

The foal's head was still bobbing around, but she started moving her legs. We watched as she scrabbled around with her front legs for a bit, then rested, then scrabbled some more. She tried to stand, first

pushing up with her front legs, then with her back legs. She fell over a couple of times, but finally managed to stand up on her own.

I looked over at Moonpearl and Dr. B. Moonpearl was making lots of little grunts. I couldn't see what Dr. B. was doing, but she looked worried.

"What's wrong?" I asked.

"This foal was stuck, but I think I've got it now," she said. She wrapped a towel around the foal's legs and pulled, long and steady. Nothing moved for a few moments, then Moonpearl gave a big heave and the second baby came out. Dr. B. began cleaning up the baby. This foal was a lot smaller than the first one, but was white like Moonpearl.

Moonpearl rolled over and stood up. She turned around and saw her babies. She nudged the first one with her nose. The foal took a few steps, swaying on those long spidery legs. A few more steps and she began poking her nose around Moonpearl's side, looking for milk.

"Allegra, I need more towels," Dr. B. said. Allegra hopped up and ran out of the stall. Dr. B. pulled the rest of the white sac off the second foal. "This one is a boy," she said.

He was very still and his eyes were closed.

"Is it OK?" I asked. I crawled over next to the foal.

"We need to get him to breathe," Dr. B. said. She took off her gloves and put on a fresh pair. Allegra handed her a towel, and she cleaned off the foal's head. She took a swab and cleared out its nostrils too. The foal still wasn't moving. Dr. B. put her hand behind the foal's front leg.

"His pulse is weak," she said.

Dr. B. handed me a towel. "Rub him down, firmly, but gently," she said. She began looking for something in her medicine box.

I rubbed the foal with the towel. He was just as warm as the first one, but so much smaller.

"Allegra, have you seen the mask and kit for intubation? It's not here," Dr. B. said.

"No, I thought you kept them in the box," she said. "Mom, is the foal going to be OK?"

Dr. B. knelt over the baby. "I hope so." She held one nostril closed and then bent her head down and blew into the other nostril several times. The foal's chest rose and fell as she did it. She stopped, and then the foal's breathing stopped.

"Allegra, you make sure that the first foal is nursing and keep them calm and out of the way. Eric, come around to this side and press down on his ribs, and count, like this." She put her hand on the baby's rib cage, just behind the front leg, and pressed down and then quickly released the pressure. "One, two, three, four, staying alive, staying alive," she said. "Now, your turn."

I pressed and counted, up and down, up and down. I could feel the ribs give just a little under my hands. I kept counting. A couple of times I thought the foal was breathing, but I didn't dare stop. Dr. B. blew into the foal's nostril again, then began rubbing its legs and neck.

Moonpearl turned to watch us. The first baby, the filly, was nursing, her little tail switching back and forth. Timothy slipped back into the stall to inspect the situation.

"Timothy, tell Moonpearl to touch the baby with her horn," I ordered, starting to feel panicky.

"Moonpearl might be too weak for that and she needs to take care of the other foal," Dr. B. said. She blew into the white foal's nose again and again.

"But it's her baby! She must want to help him," I insisted, still pressing and releasing. Moonpearl made a funny rumbling sound and tossed her head.

"She does want to help, but it won't work," said Timothy. "She says the power doesn't work on other unicorns. They can't heal each other."

Moonpearl grunted and turned toward us, the

little filly staggering a bit to try and turn with her. Moonpearl lowered her head and blew out her breath over the baby's face, then lifted up and looked me in the eye. She wanted me to save him.

It had been several minutes since the baby had been delivered. Dr. B. kept blowing into his nose, then taking a big gulp of air and blowing some more. She sat up and took his pulse again. I was afraid she was going to give up. Moonpearl was still watching us. Dr. B. shook her head and began wiping her hands off with a towel.

"He just needs to breathe!" I kept pressing and counting, then pressed a bit harder. I felt the ribs push back, just a little, and then the colt made a wet snuffly noise. I lifted my hands and the colt took a big breath. His ribs moved, then his head went back. His eyes fluttered open and he looked right at me.

CHAPTER TWENTY-ONE

"He's awake! Look, he's awake!" I cried, still pressing on the foal's ribs.

"Yes, yes, he is. Eric, you can stop the compressions now," said Dr. B. I sat back on my heels, but left my hand on the baby's ribs, feeling him breathe. Moonpearl stepped closer, nuzzling her baby's face with her nose. I scooched back to give them some room and the doctor did too. Allegra stayed by the stall door.

The colt raised his head, looking at his mom. He

scrabbled around with his front legs, then stopped, his ribs going up and down. He kicked his back legs, and rocked back and forth a couple of times before rolling up onto his chest. Bits of straw were tangled in his stubby little mane, which stood up like a rooster comb along his neck. Moonpearl blew on him to shake loose a bit of straw that was dangling over his right eye. The filly hopped over, still shaky on her skinny little stick legs, to look at her brother.

Dr. B. started rummaging around in her blue box. Keeping her voice quiet, she said, "There are still some things I need to do for Moonpearl, so we have to be calm for a bit longer. It's very important that the second foal start nursing in the next twenty minutes. I want you two to watch and if he doesn't stand soon, we will need to get some of the milk from the mother and hand feed him." She poured some solution into a little cup and got out some scissors. "If he stands on his own, Eric, you can steady him and help him to nurse. Allegra, you help me with the filly, but first, put that blanket back on Moonpearl so she won't catch a chill."

I didn't pay too much attention to them after that; I just focused on the new foal. His head was even more wobbly than his sister's, like it was too heavy for his neck. Moonpearl fussed over him a bit more. The foal rocked back and forth and got his forelegs out in front and bent at the knees. He rested for a bit, then worked on his back legs. After a few more rocks, he scrambled onto all fours and stood there trembling. He swung his head around to look at me and at his mom.

"Go on, you can do it," I whispered. "Take a step." Moonpearl tossed her head, like she was agreeing with me. The foal tried to lift a back leg, then sat down, his front legs still propping up his chest. He looked so confused, I had to laugh. After a couple more tries, he managed a few steps.

"This way, that's a good boy," I said. I got up to

help guide him to Moonpearl's side and almost pitched over myself. My knees were stiff from sitting so long and my hurt leg throbbed. The foal bumped into Moonpearl's front leg, but kept going. He wasn't as tall as his sister, and almost walked right under his

mom. He nosed around and finally started to nurse. Moonpearl gave a big sigh, like she was glad that was all over now.

Dr. B. shooed both me and Allegra out of the stall. "I just have a little bit of cleaning up to do here, and Moonpearl and her babies need some time alone," she explained.

"I've been thinking about what to name the babies," Allegra said.

"Oh, no, you aren't going to give them long names too," I said. "It should be my turn now for naming."

"Lady Shimmershine Moonpearl is a perfectly lovely name, just as lovely as she is," Allegra said with a huff. It was still a stupid name.

"Children, children, I believe the lady has the right to name her own foals," called out Timothy from his perch on the stall door. I felt my face redden at that. Moonpearl wasn't a horse, she was a unicorn. She could hear us and understand what we said, even when we weren't talking to her directly. Allegra looked a bit sorry for running her mouth.

"Sorry, Moonpearl, Timothy's right," I said. Moonpearl nickered back at me.

"The lady is gracious," Timothy replied. "She says you may give them human names that you can pronounce, as you will not be able to say their proper names."

"How about you name the colt and I name the filly," Allegra suggested. That still gave her two names to my one, but since I helped the colt to breathe, it was only fair that I should name him.

"She should be called Jewel of the Night, since she's dark, Jewel for short," Allegra said.

That wasn't too bad and gave me an idea. "His name is Gem, like in gemstone."

Timothy looked back into the stall, curling up the end of his tail and letting it fall. Moonpearl shook her head and curled up her lip. "The lady approves," he told us.

I heard Dr. B. laugh at that. She came out of the stall, and jostled Timothy so he jumped down as she swung the door closed and latched it. "Those sound like fine names, a whole family of precious things," she said. She peeled off her rubber gloves and tossed them into the trash can in the corner.

"You both did well tonight," she said, putting her hands on our shoulders. "It's late, past midnight, and we should all go to bed."

I woke up the next morning on the couch in the Brancusis' living room, tangled in a bunch of blankets. I sat up when I heard someone on the stairs. Dr. B. came in followed by my dad, who didn't look too happy with me. I thought Georgie had called to tell him I would be staying here, and I was fixing to explain, when he dropped down to his knees in front of me. He took hold of my arms.

"Eric, I've got some bad news," he started. Dad

looked rough, like he hadn't slept, and his eyes were red. "It's Mama, your grandma. She's gone."

I just stared at him, not understanding. "Gone where?"

He squeezed my arms tighter. "She passed away." He cleared his throat. "Early this morning, at the hospital. Her heart just gave out."

"No."

Dad pulled me down into his arms, tucking my head under his chin, even though Harper men aren't big on hugs.

"I don't want her to be gone," I said, hiding my face so no one could see as I started to cry.

CHAPTER TWENTY-TWO

ME AND STEVE DIDN'T go to school that day. Dad left later that morning to make arrangements. Then people started showing up with casseroles and covered dishes. Chinaberry Creek is a small town, and Grandma knew practically everybody. Steve took charge of answering the door. Soon the refrigerator was full and the house looked like a church potluck supper.

Dad got back about lunchtime, just before Georgie came over with a chocolate cake. "We are so sorry about Maggie," she said to him. "Eric, Kris and Allegra want you to know that the foals and the mare are doing just fine." She set the cake down on the dining room table.

"Maggie would have been so proud of how you saved that foal," she said, giving me a hug. It felt a bit like how Grandma hugged me before she got sick — warm and soft.

"I hadn't heard about the foals," said Dad.

"You know that horses rarely successfully bear twins. These babies were born last night, and the second one wasn't breathing at first. Eric did CPR on him while the doctor got his breathing started. He saved that colt's life," she said, beaming at me.

"So you're a baby doctor now, huh?" said Steve, punching me in the upper arm. Dad gave me a funny look as I rubbed the sore spot.

"You're right, his grandma would have been proud of him. They both always were crazy about all kinds of animals," Dad said.

After Georgie left, Dad called me over and pulled an envelope out of his jacket pocket.

"Your grandma wanted you to read this after she was gone," he said. "You might want to go to your room to read it. It's kind of private."

That struck me as a strange remark. I looked up at him.

"Do you know what it says?" I asked.

"I haven't read it, but I have a good idea," he said.

I flopped down on my bed, then slit open the envelope with my pocketknife. The page was covered with Grandma's handwriting, all shaky and spidery-looking.

Dear Eric, my favorite blue-eyed boy,

If you are reading this, I must be gone.
First I want you to know how much I love you
and all of my boys, and how proud I am of you
in particular. You are a Harper, through and
through.

I know about the white lady, that she's a
unicorn. I knew the first time you came to
see me covered in those little white hairs that
helped my aching hands.

I'm proud of how you protected her,
keeping her secret. That's why I'm leaving
Harper's Woods to you.

As you might have figured out by now, all
those rumors about a white deer over the years
weren't about deer. There are other things,
wonderful, magical things that appear in our
woods from time to time. We Harpers have

always looked out for them, kept their secret to keep them safe.

Your daddy knows about this, but not your brother. Steve's a good boy, but his path lies somewhere else and I have written to him about it. Your daddy will take good care of everything until you are old enough to take it on yourself. He doesn't love the animals the way that we do, the way your granddaddy and other Harpers who were caretakers of the woods did. He agrees with my decision to leave the woods to you.

Kris Brancusi doesn't know the Harper secret, but you can tell her, since she already knows the biggest part of it, that unicorns and suchlike are real. I knew I could sell her the farmhouse when I caught a glimpse of that silly cat with his middle missing, hanging around her office. Tell that cat he's not as sneaky as he thinks.

And tell your daddy to give you the book, too. It is in the safety deposit box. The book was started by Cletus Harper and it has notes about all the creatures that we Harpers have protected. You will need to add to it about the white lady and her babies. I already wrote about the cat.

I always knew in my heart that you would be the one.

All my love,
Grandma

I didn't rightly know what to think at first. Now the fact that Harpers had never allowed hunting on their land made total sense.

There was a knock and a creak as Dad opened my bedroom door.

"You read the letter?" he asked. I nodded. He sat down heavily on the foot of my bed and looked over at me. "I figured you might have some questions."

"Why didn't she tell me? Why didn't you tell me?"

"The family rule has always been to just tell those who need to know, usually the caretaker of the woods and at least one other. Anyone who has seen the 'visitors' gets let in on the secret, but generally, the fewer, the better," he said. "She told me soon after your grandpa died, explaining that there should always be at least two Harpers who know. I didn't believe her at first. Thought the grief was getting the better of her."

"Really?"

"Yeah, really. Then she fetched down a dog crate from upstairs, with a creature inside. It was furry and had a thick bandage around its middle. At first I thought it was just a big rabbit. Then it turned around. It's got big old long ears twitching at me and an eight-point rack of antlers growing out of its head that any white-tailed buck would be proud of. She told me it was a jackalope and that they didn't usually come this far east, being a western species. I had to believe her after that."

"What happened to the jackalope?" I asked.

"I don't rightly know; I never saw it again," he said. "I need to go over to the church, talk to the preacher about some things. You want to come?"

"No, I'll stay here with Steve."

"OK," he said, giving my foot a shake. Then he left.

I flopped back down on my bed, staring at the ceiling. I had a lot to think about.

CHAPTER TWENTY-THREE

DAD MADE ME GO TO SCHOOL the next day. It was the last week before Christmas break and there were lots of tests and stuff. As if I cared about that now. I wanted to go see the unicorns that afternoon, but I had to stay and keep company with all the relatives who were stopping by the house. There were Harpers that we hardly ever saw, some of Dad's cousins and a couple of great-aunts who talked a lot about people I didn't know who were kin to me in ways I didn't understand. Steve had more patience for all the company than Dad or I did. He even thought to set out a couple of the cakes people had brought by, along with the good plates and all. I guess Grandma would have been proud of him, too, for doing things proper.

We ate one of the noodle casseroles from the refrigerator for dinner. Afterward, we got dressed in our Sunday best. Nobody said much on the drive to the funeral home. The undertaker took us back to the room where Grandma was laid out in her coffin. There were big pictures of her set up on stands — one taken a couple of years ago, at a sort of church thing when she got an award for most years teaching Sunday school, and one of her and Poppaw and Dad, when Dad was just a kid. Dad looked to be about six or seven, with a front tooth missing. People always said Steve favored him, and I could see it in that picture, the way their ears stuck out and they had the same nose. Grandma looked young and pretty, her hair all dark and curly, and long dangly earrings framing her face.

The undertaker, Mr. Schumacher, explained how the visitation would go. People would come in to the right and sign the guest book. Then they would walk past the coffin and the pictures to where we were standing so they could "offer their condolences" to us as the immediate family. He left, closing the door behind him, to give us time to say our private good-byes.

Dad went over to the coffin first. I hung back close to the door with Steve. Dad stood there for a while, then kissed his fingers and pressed them to her cheek. He gave a big sigh.

"I'm going out for a cigarette break before everybody starts showing up. You boys going to be all right here by yourselves?" he asked. I looked up at Steve, who nodded, so I did too. Dad fished a pack of Salems out of his jacket pocket as he left the room.

We stood there by the door for a couple more minutes, not sure what to do. The last time we had been to a visitation, it was for Poppaw, four years ago. I was just a little kid and didn't remember much about it.

Steve poked me with his elbow. "Why don't you go say your goodbyes first?" I walked up to the coffin. Grandma had on her favorite Sunday suit, blue-jay blue, her head resting on a white satin pillow. They put too much makeup on her. I could tell she wasn't there anymore. She really was gone.

I glanced back at Steve—he was looking at the cards on the flower arrangements. So I took the necklace with the pendant of unicorn hair out of my pocket. I had found it in the box of her things from the hospital.

"Allegra made this for you, an extra thick one to help you get out of the hospital, remember? I guess you didn't have a chance to wear it," I whispered, as I slipped the necklace into the pocket of her jacket. "I wanted you to meet the unicorn, to make you better. Her name's Moonpearl. I'm sorry you didn't get to see her, but I promised to keep her a secret. I know

now you would have kept her secret too." My throat was getting all tight and my nose was stinging. I looked around. Steve was still on the other side of the room and Dad wasn't back yet.

"I'll take real good care of Harper's Woods. I miss you. Goodbye, Grandma." I had to go find some tissues so I could blow my nose. I tucked a bunch extra in my jacket, just in case Allegra or somebody might need some.

I went over to look at the flowers myself, to give Steve a turn. He went up to the coffin and I kept my back to him, for privacy if he needed to cry a bit, and to keep from eavesdropping.

Dad came back in at seven o'clock just as the first people arrived, some of the ladies from church. I stood between Steve and Dad, shook a lot of hands, and said "Thank you for coming" a lot.

After about twenty minutes, I told Dad my leg was about to give out, so I sat in a folding chair next to the big photos. The stitches were itching and my ankle was throbbing and I could think of about a gazillion places I would rather be than Volger's Funeral Home right that minute. Jamal and his mom came. He said Butterfinger was still doing great, was still the best dog in the world. Dr. B., Georgie, and Allegra came too.

"The foals are doing fine," said Dr. B. "Maggie would have been proud of how you helped with them. She was a remarkable woman, your grandmother. I wish I had gotten to know her better."

Allegra came up right close and I was afraid for a minute she was going to hug me, but instead she whispered, "Timothy said Moonpearl was asking where you were. She wants to see you." That made me smile.

"I'll be back tomorrow. You can tell her that."

They left, and more people shuffled down the line, so many that we didn't leave until almost eleven o'clock that night.

———

The next morning I woke up early, before anyone else. I had a piece of cherry pie, made by one of the church ladies, for breakfast. After grabbing a couple of apples, I headed over to the barn. It was one of those crisp days, when the sky seemed closer because the blue was so clear. My bad leg was pretty stiff, so I stopped and rested a few times.

Nobody else was out in the barn yet. All the better, to have some time alone with Moonpearl and her babies. She must've heard me, because she gave a little nicker when I closed the door behind me. I looked over the stall door.

Moonpearl looked different, so skinny now, but that shimmer was even stronger. She tossed her head and huffed at me, then stepped aside so I could see the foals. They were so beautiful, so perfect. They swung their big awkward heads in unison to look at me. I slipped into the stall, moving slowly so as not to scare them. There was no sign of that contrary goose, Prissy. I guess it was too crowded for her with the foals and their mom. Their big dark eyes followed me as I walked over to Moonpearl.

"Hey, beauty," I said, pulling an apple out of my pocket. I held it on the flat of my hand for her and she gently grabbed it with her teeth. I stroked her neck and breathed in that wonderful sweet earthy unicorn smell. That calm, peaceful feeling settled over me, but I was still sad about Grandma.

"I wish Grandma could have seen you; she would have loved you as much as I do," I whispered. Moonpearl swiveled her ear back toward me. "She took care of all the special creatures of the woods, too. I guess you probably already knew that."

As I stepped to the side, my bad leg was jolted and pain shot through it. The colt, Gem, had stumbled into me. He looked up at me, then gave a stiff-legged little bounce, coming even closer. He leaned against my leg, so I reached down and stroked his head. His mane was very short and bristly, but the rest of his coat was really soft. On my other side, the filly, Jewel, had started to nurse. Her tail was flipping back and forth real fast.

Moonpearl nickered again and turned to look at me. She rubbed my leg with her nose.

"She wants to know what happened to your leg," rumbled a voice behind me. Timothy rustled through the straw bedding to sit next to Moonpearl.

So I explained about twisting my ankle and getting shot. "But it's a lot better now," I assured her.

Moonpearl looked at Timothy. "Do you think it wise, my lady?" he asked. She rolled her eyes at him. She stepped up, pushing the colt away from me. When he took a couple of steps back, she dropped her head and laid her horn across my left leg. Soft light flowed down her horn, and that weird humming sensation filled the air. I felt something wash over me, like a hot shower on a cold day. I don't have the right words to describe being touched by a unicorn horn. It made the hair on my arms and neck stand up, but not in a scary, goosebumpy kind of way. The pain was gone from my leg and ankle. Even the cut on my chin quit stinging. I bent my knee and flopped my leg around. I couldn't even feel any stretching or itching from the stitches.

I threw my arms around her neck and hugged her. "Thank you!"

"She wanted to thank you properly for all your kindness and for helping revive her colt," Timothy explained.

"You didn't need to," I told Moonpearl. "I was happy to take care of you and to help Gem. I couldn't let him die." Gem hopped back over to his mom, and tried pushing his sister away so he could nurse. She didn't stop, just stepped to the side to make room for him.

I went to fetch the curry combs and came back and groomed Moonpearl. Her sides were now much smaller, and firmer than I expected after being so stretched out. It felt great being surrounded by these beautiful creatures. I thought about Grandma and felt a stab of grief, and my eyes stung.

"How come I still feel so sad?" I wondered out loud.

Moonpearl snorted a bit. I began combing out her mane, carefully collecting the loose hairs.

"The lady said that not even she can heal a broken heart right away. Grief takes its own time to unfold," said Timothy.

"I guess it does." The foals had finished nursing and were bouncing around with their funny little stiff-legged strides. They were about the size of a skinny, long-legged breed of dog, like a greyhound, but much cuter.

I heard the barn door slide open. Allegra came in, followed by Dr. B., who was carrying her blue box of medical stuff.

"Hey, Eric," said Allegra. "Aren't they the cutest things?"

"I guess," I said. I didn't admit I had just been thinking the same thing.

"Just checking that everyone is still doing well," said Dr. B. She took some measurements of the foals, then listened to their hearts and to Moonpearl's too. I went to fetch some fresh water and Allegra got a bucket of feed.

It was right nice, all of us working together, taking care of the unicorns.

Dr. B. stood up and moved where Moonpearl could see her. "All three of you are perfectly healthy. You can go home whenever you are ready," she said.

I dropped the bucket, splashing water over my newly healed leg.

"Home? But this is their home, this is where the babies were born. They don't need to go, ever," I said. It wasn't fair. What with Grandma dying, and our saving the baby unicorn, they couldn't leave.

I couldn't bear for them to leave.

"Eric, we all knew this was coming. I know this is hard for you, especially now," said Dr. B., in her soft voice, the one that I now knew was her bad news voice. It must be the voice she used to tell people that their pets were dead, or would be soon.

Moonpearl nickered, looking at me with her greeny-brown eyes. She carefully picked her way out of the stall into the main floor of the barn and over to me. The foals followed her, first Jewel, then Gem.

"Don't leave. Please, don't leave," I whispered.

Moonpearl snorted at me and rested her chin on the top of my shoulder for a minute. That unicorn smell washed over me, and even though my heart was cracking, some of that peaceful feeling soaked in too. I hugged her neck tight. I felt the foals bumping around my legs.

"Can't they stay a little bit longer?" Allegra said in a small voice.

"It's not our decision, sweetheart," said Dr. B. "It's Moonpearl's."

Moonpearl lifted her head and blew into my ear. I dropped my arms and stepped back, and one of my hands brushed Gem's back. He bumped his head under my hand and I rubbed his ears. I heard Allegra sniffling, and she was wiping her eyes as she came over to pet Jewel.

Moonpearl walked to the door leading to the paddock in the back and waited. She turned and nodded at Timothy.

"The lady says she will miss you too, but she needs to go home. Eric, she waited until she could say her goodbyes to you, but she is ready now. Her children need to meet the rest of the herd," Timothy said.

Dr. B. slid open the door. I followed Moonpearl out into the paddock, my hand still on Gem's head. Allegra and Jewel came trailing behind. Dr. B. stroked Moonpearl's cheek and the unicorn nudged the doctor on the arm. Dr. B. crossed the paddock and unlatched the gate that opened onto the trail into the woods. Allegra dashed past me and threw her arms around Moonpearl's neck too. If she said anything, I couldn't hear it over her crying.

Moonpearl shook her head, breaking Allegra's

hold, and rubbed her check on Allegra's arm. She turned and whinnied to her babies. She stepped out of the gate, her head held high and proud. She was so graceful, glowing in the sunlight. The foals trotted after her. The three of us — well, four if you count Timothy — stood and watched as they followed the trail into the woods, farther and farther in. Finally we could see only glimpses of white through the brush and trees and hear the leaves rustle under their hooves, until they were gone.

CHAPTER TWENTY-FOUR

Dr. B. invited us over for Christmas dinner, since we had had them over for Thanksgiving.
It was just as well, as Steve didn't have much heart
for cooking — a Harper Christmas dinner that year
would have been downright pathetic. We had dinner upstairs in the farmhouse and while it still felt
strange with all the changes, nobody wanted to talk
much about the biggest change, about Grandma being gone.

Timothy helped a bit, although not in the way he
intended. He jumped up onto the table after it was

set, to snag a piece of ham. Dad hollered at him so loud, we all jumped. It scared the patients still in the clinic downstairs — the two dogs started barking and the pet duck with the broken leg started quacking. That set the rest of us to laughing. The animals carried on for a good ten minutes. Timothy hid somewhere for the rest of the evening.

Grandma was buried next to Poppaw in the churchyard. All that winter, Dad went to visit her grave every Sunday morning. I went a couple of times, but didn't have much to say.

Dad gave me the Harper book the day after Christmas. "It didn't seem right to give it to you as a Christmas present. Didn't want Steve asking questions either, so keep it hidden, OK?" he said. Steve had gotten a book from Grandma for Christmas — her recipe book, a little green cloth-covered binder with handwritten pages and recipes clipped out of the newspaper. He spent part of every Sunday afternoon cooking two or three dishes we would eat during the week.

The Harper book was big, about the size of a laptop computer. It had a black leather cover, like an old Bible, and the pages were thick and yellowed. There were lots of entries, in different handwriting, each one with a date and signature. Most of them were hard to read, what with the fancy cursive and some strange spellings. There were drawings on a few of the entries, especially the ones from my great-great-grandmother, Lillian Harper. Some of them were about seeing the creatures in the woods; some of them were about taking the creatures in when they were hurt and helping them get better. Old Cletus Harper's last entry was about seeing a unicorn, although not up close, like I had. I had so much to write about — Moonpearl, her babies, the squonk, the wampus cat, Timothy.

I found Grandma's entry about the jackalope.

Lonnie Carson's red tick hound chased a creature out of the woods that hid under the back porch. So I chased off the dog, and crawled under the porch to see what it was. It was one of the funnier-looking creatures, a trembling rabbit that still had the nerve to swipe at me with its little antlers. It had a gash on its right side, where the dog bit it. I managed to get hold of it and bandage it up. Found out it was called a jackalope.

After three weeks, it had improved enough. I took it to the pond and let it go.

I kept working at the clinic. The squonk was still there, and I added a cup of water to its jar every

Friday. I never did see it, but Allegra said they heard it singing sometimes late at night.

The rosebushes in front of the farmhouse grew like crazy, climbing up and curling along the porch rails. Georgie had had me spread the unicorn manure around the bushes, saying it would probably work as well as the cow manure from the hardware store. I guess it wasn't too surprising that unicorn poop would help plants grow so big and healthy. The rose smell reminded me of Moonpearl, and I took a big bunch of them to put on Grandma's grave at Easter.

One evening in late spring, I was going back to my house, walking along the ridge. It was that pretty time, when the sun has just gone down and everything looks soft around the edges. I heard a rustling in the brush up ahead where the trail started to curve down just past my treehouse. I thought I caught a glimpse of something white moving in the bushes. I couldn't help hoping it was Moonpearl.

I heard some leaves shushing, so I stopped, holding my breath. A white shape, glowing in the twilight, slipped past a clump of bramble. I felt a stab of disappointment—the shape was too small to be Moonpearl. It stepped out of the brush onto the path. Then I saw a little horn rising a couple of inches above his ears. It was a unicorn all right. It was Gem, coming back to me.

ACKNOWLEDGMENTS

Annie Dillard once wrote that a book is a thing that takes two to ten years to write. This book would have taken even longer without the help of so many people whom I am happy to thank here.

First, my daughters: Emily Harper Deahl provided the initial inspiration with her comment, "Unicorns are hard to treat, you know, because of their horns," and Claire Carson Deahl provided early encouragement by demanding to read fresh pages right after school.

Dr. Bobby Schopler, wildlife veterinarian at the Duke University Lemur Center, discussed possible treatments, shared horse and cow birthing stories, read the manuscript, and corrected my medical mistakes. My volunteer stint at the Piedmont Wildlife Center provided invaluable background information.

Becky Lallier shared the perfect writing retreat: a house at the lake with no phone or Internet and good company, including Anne Beardsley and Brett Batchelder. Thanks to my early readers, Zachary and Lauren Ogburn and Lia Willow Ogburn. Thanks to Frances Woods for telling me it was good, and to the rest of the Coven: Luli Gray and Louise Hawes. Thanks to Clare Reece-Glore and Susan Vann for reading the manuscript for horse sense. To the local children's book community, including the Writers and Illustrators of North Carolina (WINC) and Stephen Messer, for realizing that adult beverages and children's book writers are a great pairing, and to the Wilde reading group, for keeping me up on current books.

My editor, Kate O'Sullivan, kept the flame alive for years after I first sent her a few ragged pages. Novels are a marathon, and my previous books had been picture books, the writing equivalent of the hundred-yard dash. I couldn't ask for a better coach. Kate also found the wonderful Rebecca Green to illustrate the story. It's a wonder and a privilege to see how my words are translated into another art form.

Finally, thanks to my husband, Ben Deahl, for his long patience, and for holding down the fort while I am off in the clouds.